TANGLED TODEATH

TANGLED TO DEATH

J.M. GRIFFIN

TANGLED TO DEATH

Typesetting by Hale Author Services

ISBN-13: 978-1480270831
ISBN-10: 1480270830

Dedication

For John and Mikey
You're always there, especially when I need it most.
Love You More

Chapter 1

SOAKED WITH SWEAT, I awoke with a start. My clammy pajamas clung to my cold skin. Again. *The dream* did this. The results were always the same. I'd awaken shaking and drenched, then be overtaken by a bad case of impending doom.

A splash of water and some fresh air usually helped clear my head. I flung the blankets aside and scrambled from the bed into the bathroom. Cupping my hands under the tap, and splashing, I rinsed my face and gently rubbed my skin. The moisture soothed and awakened me completely.

Appalled at the reflection in the oval mirror above the sink, I stared at the length of shaggy brown hair that usually curved at my jaw line but now stood on end, splayed in all directions. Though it looked pale, my peach-colored skin normally glowed with health. Against the deep gray-blue of my eyes, I appeared haunted. In other words, I looked like crap.

As I opened the window an inch or two and inhaled fresh end-of-winter air, a strong sense of composure spread through me.

New Hampshire is often frigid in late March. Temperatures can linger around single digits one day and offer t-shirt weather the next. The cold, chilling draft filled the bathroom. Goose bumps formed on my skin in its wake. Hurriedly, I closed the window and then wrapped up in the fleece bathrobe that hung behind the door.

Sunshine glistened across snow-covered, Schmitz Landing — the mid-size town of less than ten thousand residents, I'd moved to several months ago. Zillions of ice crystals sparkled in the front yard. I admired their beauty from the second-floor window of my bedroom. My home was adjacent to the village green in the center of town. Birds hopped about, pecking at invisible goodies. *What were they eating?*

Traffic bustled and pedestrians hurried along the sidewalks of the neat Switzerland-like tourist town as I gazed out over the square. When the alarm clock sounded, I slapped the off button. I'd better get a move on, and try to face the day in a positive way even though *the dream* had left me cloaked in gloom.

The nightmare hadn't visited in some time, but it usually preceded what turned out to be a day I wouldn't enjoy in the least. I wondered if this would be one of those.

Jasmine, a mostly black cat with smudges of white under her chin and on her paws, stared at me from the mound of blankets. Her luminous, bright green eyes were intense and steady. One paw stretched out and the other followed as she began her yoga moves. When she arched her back, I swept the bed covers in place and fluffed the pillows. It was time to start a new day in the Tangled Wings Studio.

With an indignant demeanor, Jasmine flicked the tip of her tail and strode from the room. She'd become a spoiled feline, catered to by the studio students and by me. Even so, I appreciated her company after classes and during long evenings. I chuckled at the snooty tilt of her head before she disappeared past the edge of the doorway leading to the staircase.

After a quick shower, I donned a warm — some might say mismatched — outfit of green corduroy slacks, topped by an orange jersey and a fuchsia pink cardigan. Fashion style and colored coordinates didn't mean all that much to me.

In the kitchen, the coffee maker brewed, emitting a mouth-watering scent. I pulled a mug from the cupboard.

The Schmitz Landing Daily, a local rag, had to have arrived by now. Not exactly of *The New York Times* variety, this town's and surrounding towns' happenings kept those of us who cared, informed. My advertisement for the upcoming gallery show of work executed by the students was scheduled to be in today's issue.

Boots on, I shrugged into a jacket and headed for the front gate. Snow had fallen during the night, leaving crusted white swells that covered the steps and porch.

Even though the sun was warm and making short work of melting the freshly fallen snow, I used a shovel propped next to the studio entry to scrape snow from the deck and down the stairs. Working on the path near the furthest end of the L-side of the house, I spotted a lumpy mound atop the wrought iron bench nestled at the corner a couple feet away from where I stood. Startled by the size of the heap, I shaded my eyes from the sun and leaned closer, wondering if a jacket sleeve really peeked out on the left side. Aghast, I pushed that idea away.

The shape rattled me though, and the shakes I'd had earlier returned. Rooted to the spot, my legs refused to move when I tried to step forward. Grumbling, I grunted in disgust and used the long handle of the shovel to prod and poke the large mass a couple of times. Chunks of snow cascaded down the body — a real body, of a real person — frozen on my settee, in my front yard.

I gasped and stumbled backward then ran for the house. I entered the house after I tripped up the steps. Once inside, I whipped the phone off the counter just inside the studio. My fingers shook as I punched in the police department's number listed on the wall along with the fire department and hospital. A bored voice answered the call.

"Corporal Hanson, how can I help you?"

I drew a deep breath in an effort to sound normal instead of hysterical. *Why?* I can't say. Maybe I thought I'd relax enough to get the words out. I don't think I quite managed the relaxation thing.

"A d-dead b-body is on the bench in my front yard. You have to come over immediately," I blurted out, and hung up.

Panic steamrolled over my nerves.

I returned to the bench to wait and ensure the body was still there, that it was not a figment of my imagination. Surely someone would arrive soon?

Chilled, I buried my hands in my jacket pockets. The shaking refused to cease, even though the temperature had little to do with my initial reaction. Clouds formed when I exhaled and I stamped my feet to stay warm, all the while wondering why no one had shown up yet.

It didn't occur to me until much later — when Detective Jonah Kilbride mentioned it more than once — that I'd omitted my location when I'd made the call.

After a long wait, sirens sounded. The noise level increased by the second. A cruiser halted at the gate followed by a rescue vehicle. A ruggedly handsome man approached. A police badge, attached to his jacket pocket, flashed in the sunlight as emergency personnel emerged from the rescue vehicle.

The officer held them at bay, stating he needed to assess the situation before they trampled it. Astonished and nerve-wracked after finding a person frozen to death, I waited in silence.

His ocean-blue eyes swept over me with a glance. He acknowledged me with a brief nod and asked if I had made the call.

"While clearing the walk, this caught my eye," I admitted and motioned to the mound. "I poked it with the shovel handle, and the snow fell, revealing someone underneath."

The tall man with a cropped thatch of brown hair and C-shaped scar that ran from the end of his left eyebrow to the corner of that eye, held my attention as unbidden tears dribbled down my cheeks and froze. I looked away, steadied my nerves and sucked in a deep breath.

Before he turned to the bench, he introduced himself as Detective Jonah Kilbride. He looked me over, and mentioned I was probably in shock and ordered me to go inside.

To say I don't take orders well is an understatement. I resist being bossed around, even if the advice is well-intended. As though I'd taken his advice, I retreated a few steps until his attention turned to the body. Curious, I sidled nearer and leaned over his shoulder as he assessed the body.

He stiffened and gave me a testy glare.

"Weren't you going indoors? You're cold and have icicles on your chin."

I brushed at them with stiff, chilled fingers, and tucked my hands into my pockets. Without a word, I gawked at the victim.

Exposed to the sun, leftover snow had loosened. My mouth hung open. I sucked in a deep breath when the particles fell off her face. Drool gathered on my bottom lip. Holy moly, I recognized the woman.

I gulped. Words exploded from my mouth. "Oh, gosh, that's Flora Middly." I slapped my hand against my lips to stem the flow of words, but it was too late.

His rich-colored gaze landed on me and there was a question in their deep depths. Kilbride's brows jacked up a notch.

"You know this woman? Is she a friend of yours?"

Flora's double chin sagged to her chest. Her pouched cheeks were no longer florid. Her mean-spirited, empty-of-life, sea-weed-brown bug eyes were nearly closed. My head bobbed up and down like a bobble doll in answer to Kilbride's questions.

I turned my back on Flora. Even though she'd been hardcore miserable, I found the thought of her death difficult to bear.

"She's not exactly a friend. She was more of a nuisance than anything, but she didn't deserve to die." I paid attention to his face, a face that gave nothing away. "Do you think she suffered a heart attack or something?"

"Go inside … Ms?"

"Oh, uh, Katie Greer." Startled by his cool tone, I shuffled my feet a bit. "Sorry. Yes, I'll go in now." I stumbled up the path into the house. I stood at the window and followed the progress as the team bagged, tagged, and took Flora away. The stretcher tilted and swayed over the uneven cobblestones. My stomach rolled as they wheeled her over the leftover snow, now turned to puddles of slush from the tramping of multiple boots.

The brute gazed after them before heading toward the studio. He climbed the three short stairs in one stride and peered at me through the glass while I stared back. He motioned for me to let him in. With a catch in my throat, I did so. Damn, *the dream* had indeed flung this nastiness upon me.

When he finished stamping clumps of snow and slush from his booted feet, I suggested he join me in the kitchen. I hadn't even had coffee yet or managed to retrieve the newspaper.

Waiting for him to follow me, I realized I ought to gather my thoughts before the questions began. I'd been questioned in the past. The memories of that part of my past sprang to mind. I briskly tucked them in the compartment in my brain labeled *bad times*.

Detective Kilbride gazed around, taking in the finished artworks, those in progress, and the cat balanced primly on top of the cash register. He reached out to her.

Jasmine sniffed his fingers and allowed him to scratch her ears. She promptly offered her stamp of approval with a loud purr. The corners of his mouth tilted up at Jasmine's pleasure as we moved on to the kitchen.

I poured coffee with a shaky hand. Kilbride leaned against the counter and watched my every move. He smiled slightly and nodded when I lifted a cup in his direction. His attention moved to the room — Kilbride's steady gaze missed nothing. No doubt he memorized the details.

He withdrew a small notepad from the inner pocket of his jacket.

Wary, I waited for him to speak.

"Ms. Greer, how long have you been a resident here?"

"Almost a year. Why?"

He waved a hand toward the classroom and ignored my question. "This business … Do you have a good following? Was Flora Middly one of your students?" Again, his face gave nothing away and his voice remained impersonal. I was sure he won at poker all the time.

Remembering Flora's busybody nature and wicked temperament, her criticism, and her innuendos concerning the studio and my background, I pushed the memories away and looked the detective in the eyes.

"Flora didn't attend classes. She came to an art show once, though." I left out her continued harassment of those who learned and enjoyed tangling, a form of illustration similar to, but more intense than, doodling. Tangling allowed one's mind, body, and spirit to relax and enter a yoga-ish state of mind while artists drew.

But tangling had proven to be an extreme and foreign concept for Flora.

Flora endeavored to block my business from opening and spent the majority of her time advising others not to waste their efforts on *art that made no sense*. Though it was foolish to deny my unhappiness over her abuse, I somehow managed to ignore it. I had faith she'd find someone else to irritate.

"Why did you decide to settle here?"

"While on vacation, I read an ad for Schmitz Landing and this place. It was for sale at the time, so I took the opportunity to visit and take a tour." I waved my hand around the room. "It was love at first sight. I made an offer and we moved in. The cat and I, that is. And you? How long have you lived here, Detective?"

His mouth sensual, he smiled full on. Square, white teeth gleamed against his tanned skin. If asked, I'd say he enjoyed being outdoors. All planes and angles, his face sported a firm chin and straight nose. Kilbride was handsome — not overly, but in a rugged way. From an artistic viewpoint, his features fascinated me, as did his scar. I wondered at the humorous glint in his eyes while he contemplated the question.

"Long enough, Ms. Greer. Long enough."

"I was just wondering. You don't have a New Hampshire accent."

He hesitated for a mere second and then said, "New York City, if you must know. Where are you originally from?"

Aware I'd opened myself up for his question, I'd been caught in my own trap. I didn't want to tell him, for fear he would poke into my background. Nobody needed to know about that. Too late to consider the consequences of my own stupidity, I answered him.

"The Midwest," I said and then asked, "More coffee?"

"Sure, thanks." He offered his empty cup before settling into a chair, as if he had nothing pressing to do.

"It appears someone strangled Ms. Middly using a leather belt decorated with distinct artwork resembling art in your studio. Do you have any idea where this particular material might be available? It doesn't have belt holes or a buckle, but is just a plain strip of leather."

Panic threatened to overtake me. Worried I'd become suspect number one, even though I didn't have leather of any type in the studio for students to work on, I sipped my coffee to bide time and then shook my head.

"Some of the students, and even I, work on a variety of surfaces, but not leather."

"Forensics will be handled at the state level, but when the evidence comes back, I'll have more questions. You aren't planning a trip are you?"

"I have a business to run, Detective." Duh! Where did he think I would go, on a vacation to Florida, or the Caribbean? Though an enticing thought, I knew I belonged here.

Detective Kilbride rose, adjusted his jacket and said, "Good. Glad to hear it. By the way, do you know of anyone with a grudge against Ms. Middly?" His question, shot off in a nonchalant manner, set my teeth on edge.

"While she made herself unlikeable, I can't think of one single person who would want to do away with her." I shuddered. "What a horrible way to die."

His blue eyes, cold, he muttered, "There's no good way to die, Ms Greer." He dipped his head and left me standing in the kitchen with Jasmine, rubbing against my leg, demanding a snack.

Chapter 2

A CHIME SIGNALED the opening of the studio door. Musical notes permeated the house. The events of earlier that morning lay heavy on my mind. I'd managed to feed Jasmine, fill her water bowl, and then add a splash of makeup to my still too-pale face before the students arrived.

After adding a touch of lip color, I rushed through the hallway connecting my living quarters to the studio and gallery, in time to see Francine Cross and Freda Grace enter. A gust of wind followed them in. Both women had questioning expressions on their faces as they hung their jackets on pegs near the door.

Francine, a tall, reedy, nervous sort, stepped forward, her hands all aflutter. "Was Flora Middly really frozen on your bench?"

She'd gotten the question out when Freda, a kind and wise, late-sixty-something woman who walked with a cane, reached over and clasped my hand, "You must be a wreck, dear," she sympathized. "You poor darling, what a shock."

I agreed, with a nod. "Yes, it was. Because of the snow, I didn't recognize her at first." I motioned them toward seats. "Would either of you like a cup of tea before we start? I'm uncertain whether the others will attend class today."

Francine smirked. "Don't you worry, they'll be here. Not only for class, but they'll want the scoop on Flora."

The door chimed again as I set the electric tea kettle to boil. Gretchen Winters, a twenty-eight-year-old hairdresser rushed in with the latest gossip, followed by Bill Creech and Brenna

Pestler. Bill, a mid-forties man, currently worked through the final stages of grief over his wife's death. His intense dislike for Flora had shown itself on a variety of occasions.

Brenna — whose gregarious personality and high energy level had brought her to the studio on orders from her physician — had bright, light-brown eyes and a contagious smile. She was a short, stout woman with a round face. Her coarse orange hair sprung out from her head, antennae-like, giving the appearance of someone whose body ran on static electricity. I grinned at Brenna.

She settled at the table and immediately lined up her blending stump, pencil, and pens, soldier-like in front of her.

"Flora Middly has been a pain in the rear since I can remember, but she shouldn't have died like that. No sirree," Brenna stated in a matter-of-fact tone.

Gretchen lifted mugs off the pegboard above the kettle. Though she wore a sly smile, she uttered not a word. When the tea container had made the rounds, Gretchen poured piping-hot water into each cup. When I caught her brown-eyed wink at me, I realized Gretchen knew something about Flora.

General murmurs of agreement with Brenna's statement crossed the room, and mine joined them. We sipped our brew and started the usual breathing relaxation ritual before they initiated work on individual projects. A palpable silence ensued until broken by the entrance of Janet Latchkey, who consistently arrived last.

A late afternoon-into-evening waitress in the local diner across the square, Janet was smart, savvy, and could be a bit snarky on occasion. She also held a soft spot for Bill, which meant that underneath all the snarkiness, beat a gentle heart. She disliked Flora, but had never explained why. I wondered about that as I hung her coat on the remaining peg.

After we discussed how and where I'd found Flora, I asked them not to dwell on the incident. Looks passed back and forth, but everyone agreed and set to work again.

Janet stated, "I want to say this before we get started. Flora

Middly's rotten busybody attitude meant trouble for all those she ran across. I, for one, am not sorry she's gone from this earth." Cheeks pouched, Janet blew a breath through pursed lips and defiantly added, "I've said what you're all probably thinking, except for you, Freda. You never think poorly of anyone." She gave Freda a huge smile, patted her hand, and began to tangle a new tile.

Each of them had initially come to class for one reason or another, but mostly for relief from the stress in their lives. When I first opened for business, I'd feared nobody would be willing to participate in this art style. I had Flora to thank for those feelings of fear and anxiety.

I'd done the necessary and obligatory free demonstrations and even taught a class at the elementary school. After a class at the local wellness center, the participants handed out brochures and recommended my business. I returned the favor by attending yoga classes to generate well-being of my own. It had helped me deal with my recurring dream.

Silent and meditative, the artwork took shape. We broke to stretch and chat. I used the time to peruse the various projects and was pleased at the efforts made. Gretchen approached me after Bill entered the restroom located at the far end of the studio.

She whispered, "I want to share something with you, but not now. Let's get together later."

"Sure," I murmured, "come by after work."

With a nod, Gretchen said, "My last appointment is at four. I'll be here after I've finished up. You don't mind?"

"Not at all. I'll make supper, unless you're engaged elsewhere tonight?"

"Ooh, I'd appreciate a meal, thanks," Gretchen answered. Then with a wide smile she wandered off to speak with Freda.

The remainder of the morning passed in silence. With their work stored, the students purchased supplies for upcoming projects. I listened to them discuss the gallery show scheduled for the next week.

"You still gonna hold the opening, Katie?" Bill asked.

He'd worked so hard — disappointment wasn't an option.

"Of course," I assured him. "Was my ad in today's newspaper? I haven't retrieved mine yet. Finding Flora ... well enough said."

"I'll get it for you," Brenna offered and scooted out the door without her jacket.

Francine chuckled at Brenna's quick response and remarked, "We think it's a nice advertisement. Did you manage the layout yourself or did Jenkins generate the graphics for you?"

Ray Jenkins, the sole reporter for the *Schmitz Landing Daily* — which only published every other day since cutbacks at the paper took place — was a news correspondent come graphic designer who now wore more hats than he could have imagined. Layoffs had doubled and tripled jobs performed by the few remaining employees. Internet published newspapers continued to seriously cut into profits as more people opted to read their new online. Many stalwart folks, like me, would rather read a real newspaper than get their news online.

"Jenkins kindly offered to give me a hand. He's quite good, too," I answered.

Brenna burst through the studio door like her shoes were afire. Snickers rounded the room, though nothing was said. Going through life as though constantly ablaze, Brenna often acted like tearing around would extinguish the flames, hence her need to relax.

Bill told us the page number. I found and admired the bold, captivating lettering surrounded by a decorative geometric border. Student names followed the date and time of the opening. I glanced over the page top at their happy faces and laughed aloud.

"Can we get a look at the space you intend to use?" Freda asked.

"Sure, the formal living room will now become a full-time gallery. It's enormous and perfect for this and future events." I used the studio for my own shows, but the work compiled by these people called for a larger area. I invited the group to enter through heavy double pocket doors into the house itself.

The building, an L-shaped affair, held a large room facing the street and across from the town square. A fireplace, topped by a hand-carved ornamental mantel stood centered in the outside wall. It left ample space for project displays above it and on the other walls. A Persian carpet lay atop hardwood flooring. High-backed antique chairs squatted near the perimeter of the rug.

I'd gotten rid of the ugly sofas before I moved in.

An electrician had agreed to barter his work for a watercolor picture he'd admired. The lighting he'd installed would perfectly show the work at its best. One of the handymen from the wellness center kindly positioned strips along the top edges of the wall in order to suspend framed art from cords.

The group unanimously approved of the space as they walked about, gazed at the furniture, and peered out the windows. Neighboring homes on this side of the property stood distant from mine. The acreage included in the sale offered privacy and that had sealed the deal when I looked the place over.

"Who put in your lighting?" Bill inquired.

"Joe Schmitz," I answered. "We bartered for payment. He wanted a painting I'd done last year, so I traded with him."

Bill's face took on a solemn appearance. Hastily, he checked the time and stated he had to leave, but would attend class the next day.

Confused by his abrupt change in demeanor, I watched him scoot from the room and heard the studio door close. Bill scurried along the trampled slush-laden walk without a backward glance.

Curious over his reaction, I turned to find all eyes on me and puzzled expressions on their faces.

Janet wanted to know, "What's with Bill?"

I shrugged. "I haven't a clue. He asked who did the electrical work. I mentioned Joe Schmitz's name and he flew out of here right afterward. What's going on? Are you girls aware of something I'm not?"

Looks slid between them. The women shook their heads or shrugged in answer.

"Come on, don't treat me like an outsider."

Freda, the one person I'd least expect, stepped forward. "Flora caused problems in Bill's marriage. She insinuated Bill's wife and Joe had a thing going on. It wasn't true. Bill hasn't trusted him ever since Flora did her dirty work. She relished her role as a troublemaker, you know. Look how hard she tried to stop you from opening this business. A pain in the butt, that's what she was." Freda thumped her cane on the floor for good measure.

Though surprised at Freda's words, I considered them significant since Freda refused to gossip — but first times apply to everything in life.

Janet came to Bill's defense. "If Joe didn't *sniff* around every skirt in town, Bill wouldn't have questioned his wife's faithfulness. Mary was hurt by the whole thing and then, of course, she fell ill not long after that. Bill still hasn't forgiven himself for his behavior. I believe he and Mary had a solid marriage."

"Joe doesn't *sniff* at skirts," Gretchen interjected. "He's a decent man. We've dated a few times and he's always behaved like a gentleman. Flora's unhappiness filtered into the lives of those she encountered." She gazed at Francine and murmured, "You know that better than most, don't you, Francine?"

With wide eyes, Francine glanced at each of us. Her face paled. "Everyone has problems, and Flora was no different." She wrung her hands and then slid them into her pants pockets. "She'd been a friend of mine, until . . ."

By placing a restraining hand on Francine's arm, Freda shushed her. Whatever Francine might have shared, Freda wanted her to stay mum. Aware of Francine's discomfort, I sent Gretchen a silent plea. She nodded slightly and slapped her hands together.

"This will be a fabulous gallery, Katie. I think you're on the right track." Gretchen glanced at her watch. "I'd better get to work. We'll all be back tomorrow." She herded the others from the room.

I counted on Gretchen to step in where needed. I was a new resident in town and that left me with little information on who was what, and the why of it all. The only news I had I gleaned came from the newspaper and from bits I garnered from the students in class.

The shop emptied of the last student. I watched their cautious progress across the slush-filled stones, until they reached the sidewalk. I promised myself to clear the path before the watery mixture froze and somebody slipped.

Chapter 3

WITH SHOVEL IN hand, I scraped the cobblestones clean. I huffed and puffed over the exertion, realizing I required more exercise and less sitting at the easel or drawing table. I rounded the side of the house to clear the driveway and walk to the rear entry. The entire time, clips of 'Flora memories' played in my head like a video.

My first encounter with Flora took place at the town meeting, when I'd applied for licensing to open my studio. Printed copies of a business plan, including art samples were distributed to the powers that be. I listened to open discussions and gleaned as much information as possible about Schmitz Landing politics.

Flora interrupted conversations over every agenda item listed. Most often, the town administrators sidestepped her complaints. When she couldn't be put off, they assured Flora her concerns would be considered before making their final decisions.

When my application came to the forefront, Flora loudly criticized my proposed enterprise as detrimental to the community. She ridiculed the tangled-as-art idea insisting it was a senseless technique to be introduced to the townspeople, especially the children. Astounded at her overt resistance to an art form she had little, if any, knowledge of, I'd played a waiting game.

The lead townsman, Harry Corbel, ordered her to be seated. He ran a pudgy hand over his bald pate and demanded Flora listen to the information I provided.

I made a presentation and a lengthy discussion took place with questions that I willingly answered. Flora blustered at every word. My resentment over her disrespect and her inability to consider a proven health-conscious venue for the public, grew with each *harrumph* she made.

Moments after the Q&A session, the committee voted and gave me their blessing. I sent Flora a satisfied smile and left the building.

For the first time, but not the last, I'd been the recipient of Flora Middly's nasty attitude.

I wiped sweat from my forehead as the sun headed toward the down side of the day. Finished with the job at hand, I marched the path just as the postal carrier place a bundle of mail in the box. He saluted and smiled. I waved as he moved on down the street.

Though I think of physical mail as a dying tradition, I enjoy receiving the daily oddities. Easy Internet access had hit the postal system hard. I knew because it now fought bankruptcy. Even when the only thing to arrive, other than bills, included a few of sale brochures, I usually took time for a cup of tea while I browsed the offerings. A sort of tradition of my own, I guess.

With the bundle stuffed under my arm, I trudged toward the house, purposely avoiding the death seat — that's how I perceived my bench at the moment. I'd have to decide whether to rid myself of the thought or the seat, but neither would happen today.

I headed through the studio into the soon-to-be gallery. A doorway lay at the furthest end from the front of the house and led to homier accommodations I called my cozy rooms — or the 'cozy' for short.

The sweet sitting area held a gas fireplace. That room opened to the kitchen by way of an arched doorway. The comfortable atmosphere lent itself to relaxation and a feeling of security.

Setting out teapot and cup, I realized how much I had enjoyed my new life and home until I found Flora dead on my bench.

J.M. Griffin

Wide windows stretched across the back of the house, offering a stunning view of the river and mountains beyond. My property stretched to a boat dock, showed off by a few weathered Adirondack chairs at the water's edge. As I went through the mail, I fancied sitting there when the weather allowed.

Schmitz Landing had been named after its founders. Boats that once docked at the river's edge had carried merchandise, but now the river was used only for recreational purposes.

The early 1900's boomtown days abruptly ended when trucking outgrew the need for boats. Over time, even the railroad had nose-dived into near oblivion. Schmitz Landing then became a tourists' dream. Featured in magazines, the town offered a quaint view of life straight from a Swiss village look alike.

I'd been struck by the authentic cobblestoned streets, the gingerbread trim on shops. Costumes worn by storekeepers had given me a bit of a laugh when I first drove in. I now knew the townsfolk were brilliant enough to offer the public a glimpse into a unique lifestyle.

Moments later, when the doorbell chimed, I tossed the mail aside, set my teacup on the tray, and answered the summons.

Detective Kilbride stood on the front steps. Great, my day took a sudden turn for the worse. I felt it in my bones.

With a reluctant smile, I ushered him in. "What can I do for you, Detective Kilbride?" His face held a serious expression that put me on guard.

"I have a few more questions, Ms. Greer." He glanced around the house as we entered the sitting room where the fireplace blazed, heating the comfy space. A rectangular tangle-designed floor cloth caught his immediate attention before he finally turned toward me. I motioned for him to take a seat.

"Would you care for coffee, Detective?"

"No, thanks." He motioned to my cup. "Don't let me interrupt your tea time."

His relaxation-prior-to-interrogation technique was top-notch. I had to give him credit. I'd experienced this before and knew what to expect. A cloak of trepidation draped my shoulders.

Seated in the soft chair, I rested my hands on the arms. To fidget was a sure sign of nervousness or guilt, a lesson I'd learned the hard way. "So fire away. How can I help?"

"You spoke of issues between you and Ms. Middly?"

I hesitated. "We had our moments, yes."

"Explain them if you would, Ms. Greer. Were they intense, heated maybe?"

"We had disagreements due to her uninhibited gossip concerning my business." I lifted one shoulder. "I resented her attitude."

"Is that all it was, simple resentment?" His all-seeing eyes stayed locked on my face.

I nodded. "We had a few arguments over it. She became a bit of a nuisance, but I would hardly choke her for that."

Kilbride flipped through his little notebook. "I'm told she had an ax to grind because you bought this house. Do you know why?"

"That's news to me. I have no idea. We never discussed the purchase. What have you heard?"

He ignored my question. "Did you ever inquire about the reasons for her actions and words?"

"No, I didn't. Detective, she was a busybody whose apparent dislike of her lot in life overshadowed all else."

He'd settled comfortably in the chair. His legs stretched out in relaxation mode. I'd seen this attempt to appear relaxed before, in another lifetime. The purpose of it being to create a seemingly pleasant atmosphere so the suspect in question would make a mistake. The only difference being *he* was my interrogator, and I held the status of *his* prime suspect now. That old life of mine and what followed jumped front and center into my thoughts.

I shoved the memory into the recesses of my mind and sipped the cooled tea, taking care not to rattle the cup against the saucer.

"Can you think of anyone who wanted Flora Middly dead?"

"Nobody comes to mind. I have given her murder some thought, though. Flora's constant badgering left people at a point where some even crossed the street to avoid meeting her. If she treated all the business owners in town the way she did me, I'm not surprised she's been done away with. Frankly, even my students ..."

I stopped short. The sentence hung between us.

His eyes sparkled and his face took on an animated appearance. Obviously interested, he leaned forward.

"Your students what, Ms. Greer?"

"Have their own opinions, and I have no more to say." I set the cup and saucer aside and folded my hands. "You should ask them. And please, call me Katie."

Kilbride mumbled, "I just might do that, ask them, I mean."

He lounged in the chair again, his focus on my body language. His gaze traced my form more than once before stopping on my face.

"You never mentioned exactly where you came from. The Midwest was rather vague. I checked with the realtor who sold you the house. She stated you paid cash. Do you carry such large sums of money around in a suitcase, Ms., uh, Katie?"

Amused, I laughed at his attempt to get under my skin. Better cops than him had tried and hadn't managed to do that. Why he thought himself any different piqued my interest.

Certain he had dug into my background, I retorted, "Dying to ask the real questions, aren't you, Detective? Go ahead, ask." My words sounded snarky, even to me. I clamped my mouth shut before I added something I'd regret.

He sat forward, his shrewd eyes alight. The danger I felt from them rang my internal alarm, but I could hold my own. I had before, and I would again.

He offered a wry smile. "If you insist, I will. Why leave Columbus? Why come here? Not because you were on vacation, but because you wanted to outrun your past ... Am I right?"

I inclined my head. "Close. Very close. Everyone deserves a

new beginning, don't you agree, *Mr. I'm-from-New York*? What prompted you to leave the Big Apple?"

Kilbride's eyes darkened. His face stiffened.

In a harsher voice, he said, "I'll ask the questions. It's none of your concern why I left New York City."

"My point, exactly. It's none of your business why I left Ohio."

He smirked at my answer. The scar crinkled at the corner of his eye, lending a lopsided appearance to his eyebrow. I noticed he rubbed the length of the scar when he was deep in thought.

"I'm aware of your identity and what happened. Did you think I wouldn't find out?" Kilbride inquired.

"I wasn't hiding secrets from you. My life is an open book." I lied and measured his attitude and body language. "By the way, what *have* you found out?"

He flipped a couple pages of his petite booklet and read, "You're twenty-four and come from a wealthy artistic family that lived in a well-to-do suburb of Columbus. Your name isn't Katie Greer, but is Katarina Granger. Your parents were murdered, leaving you the main suspect. You'd been hospitalized with wounds inflicted by either you or the would-be killer." He glanced up, measured me with those gorgeous blue eyes, and then continued.

"You're unable to recall how your parents' deaths occurred or how you received your injuries. That fueled an investigation." He slapped the pages shut and asked, "How did you get out of it?"

I slid to the edge of the chair cushion. Goaded by his accusation of guilt, I snapped, "First off, I didn't kill them. Secondly, I'm not violent. And third, a damn good lawyer put the detective in charge to shame. Not one shred of evidence availed itself as proof that I committed murder, and there was no reason why I would. I adored my parents. We did everything together. They nurtured my talent, and I suffered terribly after they died." I fought to keep my rising voice and anger under control.

His expression shuttered, he murmured, "Ah, but you were left well-off. Money is always a motive."

I swallowed a renewed spurt of anger that threatened to overflow. "Kilbride, you haven't quite managed to delve deep enough. If you had, you'd understand I'd been a rising star in the art world. I had money, more than I needed, from sales of my art alone. My grandmother left me well-off when she passed away. There was no reason to kill my parents for financial gain." I waved a hand as he opened his mouth. "Furthermore, I paid for this house using inheritance money from Grandma."

I lowered the fireplace thermostat and turned to find Kilbride checking his notes again. I itched to take a look at them.

"If we're finished, I have an appointment." I dismissed him with a flick of my hand and an intentional note of boredom in my voice.

Though pique darkened his eyes, danger glittered within their deep blue depths. I'd hit a nerve and that satisfied me to no end. Two could play hardball, and this time around, I refused to be the victim of some sick bastard's crime.

"You look all sweetness and light, but you're a tough one, aren't you?" Kilbride tipped his head to the left. "As a suspect, I suppose you've learned to protect yourself. Cops can be cruel and excessive during interrogations. Speaking of suspects, you're not alone on my list."

I snorted. "Why, Detective Kilbride, it's most comforting to know there's a list. Now get out."

He grinned, shrugged, and strode away. The studio door chime sounded as he left. I traced his steps to peer out the window after him. He reached the street and paused. He stared at the building, probably catching my movement when I drew closer to the curtain. With a smirk, he waved, entered his car, and drove off.

Gretchen would enter by way of the kitchen. I switched on exterior lights for her. I couldn't wait to hear her gossip and suppositions. The woman was a veritable beehive of information. Whether factual or wishful thinking, her customers' stories kept me entertained.

Chapter 4

THE DOORBELL CHIMED incessantly. I set the quiche on the table and raced to let Gretchen in. She stood on the doorstep stamping her feet, her coat wrapped tight around her. Her frown indicated I'd allowed her to freeze out there for too long.

I laughed, listening to her whine about the weather. When she drew a breath, in sympathy, I imitated a person playing a violin.

Her laughter mingled with mine. "Brrrr. It's so darned miserable when the sun goes down. I hope you have wine and something decent to eat. I'm starved." She flung her coat on a chair next to the fireplace in the sitting room before taking a stance in front of the flames.

I handed her the wine bottle and two goblets. "You pour. Dinner's nearly ready to eat. The menu is veggie quiche and warm bread. How's that?"

Gretchen grinned and said, "Sounds yummy. Was the hunky detective here again today?"

I chuckled. "I can tell by your face you know he was. Who told you?"

Gretchen sipped her wine and then said, "My last customer saw him arrive before she came in for her appointment. She thinks he's a scrumptious snack. Is he?"

"More like a thorn in my side than a snack." I snickered and shrugged. "He *is* handsome, if you happen to like that look."

"I must see this man."

I stared at the fire for a moment, remembering he'd said he

planned to visit my students. "I'm sure you'll have the chance. He intends to speak with each of you since you attend classes here, knew Flora, and might have had your own problems with her." I set the wine glass aside and finished preparing the meal. I sliced warm bread and filled a small bowl with rich honeyed butter.

I called to Gretchen to join me and motioned her to the seat across the table from mine.

"It's a simple but nourishing dish." With that, I offered her the fare.

We ate as though we'd starved ourselves for months. Teasing, I bickered with her over the last slice of bread and butter until I sliced more and refilled the bowl with the butter mixture.

Replete, we took the wine bottle and glasses, and settled near the fireplace. The heat soothed as we nestled in our respective places, satisfied and comfortably full of food.

Gretchen looked over, a sly smile curled her lips. "I bet you want to hear what I couldn't tell you this morning, huh?"

I grinned and said, "I can't wait. Are you talking gossip or truth?"

Her nose wrinkled, but she answered with sincerity. "Truth, I think. Flora Middly was supposed to inherit this house out of the past owner's estate. I'm uncertain how it happened, but I heard she had a connection to the uncle of the previous owner. A romantic one, if you can visualize that." Gretchen's eyebrows had shot so far up her forehead they nearly melded with her hairline.

I choked on a mouthful of wine. "Let's not go that route, shall we? Tell me more about this inheritance."

Wide-eyed, her enthusiasm palpable, Gretchen warmed to the tale of Flora's passion for the widowed man whose money would take her from worker bee to the queen bee of the manor. The so-called romance took place in Flora's youth, when she was easily impressed. Apparently, she'd willingly done whatever his heart desired, while he spread rumors of her gullibility.

A sense of where the story was going left me sympathetic toward the young, innocent Flora of those days. Gretchen's explanation showed how badly people could use one another.

I raised my hand in a stop motion and requested a synopsis of Flora's past. "Please don't make me feel sorry for Flora, especially after the way she treated me."

"Okay, okay, the backstory's important so you'll realize why she developed such miserable traits." Gretchen sipped the fresh glass of wine I'd handed her and continued by saying Flora ordered a wedding gown in anticipation of upcoming nuptials. She spread the word a proposal was imminent, until a neighbor took Flora aside and shared the gossip surrounding Flora and her lover.

I learned, that humiliated, Flora made a grandstand with the man, forcing him to admit he had misused her. In the end, he promised to make her the owner of the house, more out of guilt than anything. Two years later he died in an accident. Apparently, to Flora's surprise and dismay, the house passed to a young cousin and his family. When their children entered college, the couple moved away. They listed the house with the realtor and that's when I bought it.

"That experience initiated her bitterness." Gretchen unfolded her legs and rose from the chair. "If it had been me, I'd have sued for his false promises, but in those days nobody resorted to the lawsuits so common today."

I snorted, knowing she would have done more than file a suit. She'd probably have applied a swift punch to his jaw. I liked that most about her. Gretchen Winters didn't take any crap from anyone. Sort of how I'd turned out, I guess. And mine had been no easy path. Fleetingly, I wondered what circumstances had made Gretchen that way.

"So who was the neighbor who took Flora aside and explained the gossip running rampant about her?"

Gretchen smiled. I could tell she'd been waiting for the question. "Freda Grace was the one. Flora never forgave her for telling her, either."

With a low whistle, I wondered if Flora and Freda had been involved in a bitter and hateful relationship.

J.M. Griffin

"Tell me what the cop wanted today? Does he intend to question all of us any time soon?" Gretchen inquired, bright-eyed with anticipation.

"Don't sound so happy. He's not as charming as you think. He's a looker, but a cop all the same."

Her swift glance warned me to control my opinions or there'd questions. No one needed to know about me, not ever. I didn't want their pity over losing my parents, nor did I wish to be known as *the family member who survived.*

"Kilbride will want to hear your alibi during the time of Flora's death, right? What time did she die, by the way?"

"He's waiting for the coroner's report. I know the bench was empty before I went to bed. I put mail in the post box on the corner prior to …" I thought for a second and said, "Ten o'clock or so. The morning snow didn't show any footprints, either."

Gretchen leaned forward, her expression intense. "The snow started around one in the morning. My boss and I were on our way home from dinner and a theater play in Lindley." She sighed. "We drove right by this house."

I glanced outside as Gretchen stretched, yawned, and declared it was time to go. From the way ice glazed the windowpanes, I knew temperatures had become increasingly frigid by the hour. I stacked dinner dishes in the dishwasher as Gretchen buttoned her coat and wound a bulky scarf around her neck.

Walking through the house into the studio, we headed to the front gate where I watched her stride the two blocks to her apartment above the bakery. Aware safety was an issue, I waited until she entered.

With my thoughts on Flora Middly, I hurried past the bench. I shivered and rushed indoors out of the darkness and cold. I couldn't imagine being strangled to death. Kilbride was right. There wasn't a good way to die. I pushed away thoughts of my parents' demise and joined Jasmine who waited patiently for me at the bottom of the stairs leading up to our bedroom. Weary, I wondered if I could get through a night without *the dream.*

Chapter 5

CLOUDS DRIFTED, LIKE cotton ball puffs, across the azure sky. After being awakened by the alarm that even the cat disliked, I lazed in bed admiring the sun streaming in through the sheer curtains. In a snit, Jasmine left the room because I flipped the comforter aside. She often lounged deep in its warmth. I wondered what the day would bring.

Breakfast, a small affair, consisted mainly of yogurt and fresh fruit. I tossed the container in the sink with a mental note to wash it and add it to the recycling bin later. Jasmine crunched her way through a bowl of cat nibbles, sipping water in-between. I watched her begin a daily freshen-up routine and knew I needed to do the same in order for class to start on time. Once finished washing her face and paws, the cat pranced up the stairs ahead of me.

I'd taken two steps upward when hammering on the back door brought me back down. Annoyed at the early interruption of what would be a busy day, I headed for the door. Clasping my robe together, I stared out at Detective Kilbride. *What did he want now?*

My face must have expressed my thoughts, because his grin turned sheepish. I let him in and snapped, "Do you think you could return later?"

His hands raised to ward off a possible attack. "Sure, would after class work? I just thought you'd be up early," he said.

I'd been cranky and felt a fleeting second or two of remorse for my reaction. "Come in. You can have coffee and wait a few minutes while I get dressed."

This time Kilbride smiled when I mentioned coffee. He stepped further into my warm house and removed his jacket then hung it on the newel post. I handed him an empty mug and raced upstairs as Jasmine padded back down.

Her inquisitive nature meant she'd keep Kilbride entertained while I donned jeans and a heavy jersey. I slipped on my favorite pair of what used to be black leather shoes. Now they were multi-colored in metallic tones with tangled designs on them. I'd painted them and embellished the muted tones using glitter ink pens.

A soft crooning reached me as I left the last stair leading to the kitchen. I smiled at how a mere cat turned someone like Kilbride into a mushy fool. Animals will do that when you least expect them to. Jasmine had this tall, hard-bitten cop wrapped around her paw. Amused, I couldn't let the opportunity to tease him, slide.

"Jasmine has your number, Detective." I snickered at the sight of them in the chair. Jasmine lay sprawled across his lap like a blanket.

"She's a fine pet," Kilbride said as he set her on the floor and brushed cat hair from his slacks.

"She's good company, accepts me for who I am, and asks no questions."

"A little early for a verbal slap, don't you think?" He wrestled a plastic bag from the inside pocket of his coat. "Let's not battle again today."

Apprehensive, I watched him slide the bag toward me. Unwilling to touch it or its contents, I waited for him to explain.

"This is the leather belt strap from Flora Middly's neck."

I peered at the strap. "Remove it from the bag, please. I'd like to see the design better. It looks familiar."

With a brief nod, Kilbride put on gloves, then straightened the loosely rolled material and laid it out flat. I left the room, returned with a magnifying bubble, and held it just above the stylized inked pattern. In slow motion, I viewed the entire length twice.

"Turn it over," I instructed.

Without a word, Kilbride did as I asked.

Again I studied the leather through the glass. I shook my head when I saw the reverse side lay devoid of tangles or initials. When a tangle is completed, it's named and signed. I'd found no indication of one or the other on either side.

I stared into Kilbride's face. His luscious lips captured my attention. I forced myself to focus on the situation, instead of on how scrumptious a snack he was.

"This wasn't done by me or my students, that I know of. I'd say someone who doesn't know the first thing about what I teach did this."

Stunned at my words, Kilbride stared at me. He folded his arms across his chest.

Eventually he glanced at the evidence and then back at me. "You're telling me this isn't your art?"

I nodded. "That's right. This person knows nothing about the art form, but is trying to place the blame on me — or my students. Take your pick of those."

"You won't mind if I'm a bit skeptical here, will you?" Kilbride smirked.

"I'll give you the name of someone who can verify what I just said, should you require another opinion. But I'm telling you, whoever did this isn't one of my people."

His expression was sardonic. "Explain the difference between the two."

"The killer is plainly not trained in the mindful art that I teach. Here." I pointed to a spot on the strap. "The design doesn't flow. Instead, it's abrupt and crude. It isn't shaded either."

He shook his head, disbelief on his features. "You really expect me to believe it's that simple?"

I raised a shoulder in a half-shrug. "If you don't believe me, wait until the students arrive and ask them."

He stared at me for what seemed an eternity. Maybe he thought I'd reached the she's-really-nuts zone. And I was unable to fathom what went on behind those rich blue eyes. I thought he considered my views though, and might take my advice. When the doorbell chimed, I realized I'd forgotten to unlock the studio.

I raced through the corridor, and let the students in followed by my apology. Three of the six usuals cheerfully hurried inside. Discarding their jackets, they assembled their work on the tables. I guessed today would be a focus-on-tangling kind of day.

Excusing myself, I returned to fetch Kilbride and a new supply of tea bags. His stood with his back to me, staring across the yard to the river. He glanced over his shoulder as I entered the room.

"Are you gonna ask, or not?" I questioned him.

"I'm open to anything that will help, so why not? I've run into the proverbial brick wall at the moment. There's an incredible list of people with grudges against Ms. Middly. It would take forever to question them all in 'the box.'"

Ah, yes, I knew the box well. That's what cops call the interrogation room. I'd been hauled into the box so many times in the past I'd begun to wonder if I'd ever get to leave without a loss of temper, my mind, or my freedom. In the end, my attorney had made life easier for me. When threatened with another trip to the station, by cops who had *just a few more questions*, the word *lawyer* repeatedly slipped past my lips. I'd watch them cringe and took consolation from their reaction.

"I didn't see your car out front. Did you walk over from the station?"

"I was dropped off. I'll call when I need a ride back. One of the guys took my car for maintenance this morning."

"Okay, good. Wait a minute before you come in, Kilbride. They're getting ready to unwind before starting work. I won't tell them you're here, so enter through the front door."

This time spent with Kilbride had been quite different from our previous interaction. I worried if his softer approach was a ruse. Maybe he endeavored to make me relax in order to pounce on things I'd say and then misconstrue them. Another hard lesson I'd learned in Ohio.

"Sure, and call me Jonah, will you? I feel like my father when you say Kilbride." A slight lift at the corners of his mouth softened his features.

I smiled at his charm, gave myself a mental head slap, and left the room. What was I thinking? Trust a cop? Especially one who thought I'd committed murder here and in Columbus?

To say I mourned the death of my parents would be a mild statement. I'd mourned so deeply ... And my great aunt had to come to my aid while I recovered from wounds inflicted by the killer. Why I hadn't died too, was a mystery.

The cops eventually concluded I'd interrupted a robbery.

My parents were murdered in summer. My mother enjoyed fresh air and opened the windows during the day. Alarmed when she heard screaming coming from our house, our closest neighbor had summoned the police. I never knew whose screams she'd heard — mine or those of my parents. My father's most expensive artworks were gone and never were recovered, while my precious parents had been brutally torn from my life. I wondered if I'd ever recover from that horrible event.

Afterward I'd often wished I'd been put out of my misery that day, too.

Those torturous days were now far behind me, though and I refused to revisit them. *The dream* was enough to deal with. Their murder case remained open, as far as I knew. A series of doctors insisted my brain had blocked the traumatic incident to protect me from the painful reality.

My students tipped their heads up to face Kilbride when he sauntered in after a light knock on the door. Curious glances swept toward me, and I offered them the same.

"Good morning, Detective," I greeted him.

He smiled and gave a nod. His acting skills were superb and I figured he'd aced the Cop 101 class.

"Ms. Greer," Kilbride answered. "I have the leather piece found around Flora's neck. I wondered if you'd take a look at it. You are the tangle expert, are you not?"

"I wouldn't go that far, but I've been teaching the art form for some time now. Let's have a look," I said with a half-grin.

By this time, everyone had slid their square paper tiles aside. Interest, and something else, passed from person to person. What the something else was, I couldn't tell. I also didn't know from whom it had started.

When Kilbride stepped to the counter, he withdrew the bag, put on rubber gloves, and laid the belt strap out flat. The entire crew gathered round. They reminded me of a group of people peering at a new baby.

With their eyes intent on the strap, each person gawked at the design. They looked at one another and then straightened up to face Kilbride.

"This isn't real. It's somebody's idea of what tangling is," Bill exclaimed.

Freda nodded. "Looks more like doodling to me. Definitely a fake. I'm sure."

Each student scrutinized the work a second time, in search of a name somewhere on the drawing. Nothing showed itself, making them even more certain it was not authentic.

Francine told Kilbride how tangling creates art by using purposeful, repetitive marks. She added, "Tangling assists in the relaxation process of stress relief and the refocusing of one's mind, while doodling is a simply scribbles that aren't as directed. Doodling has little benefit. It merely passes the time."

Once again, Bill jumped in. "She's right, there's a distinct difference between the two." He nodded, satisfied with his own words.

Each student made their opinions clear to Kilbride in their distinct way. Proud to think all the information I'd shared with them had embedded itself, my heart swelled.

Kilbride lifted his hands in acknowledgement that he'd gotten the message. He turned to me and muttered, "You have taught them well. They are indeed immersed in the subject."

Freda thumped her cane and remarked, "Besides that, the fool didn't sign it. Everyone knows you name, date, and sign each piece."

Kilbride fought to keep the grin at bay, but it burst forth anyway. The group smiled in return, probably thinking he'd found they were right — and justifiably so.

"Thanks for your help with this. I figured I'd get some good information."

All this time, Gretchen had stood aside, watching and waiting while the others spoke. Kilbride turned to her. She smiled and nodded her head, saying she agreed with the others.

The group was about to begin working when Kilbride tucked the evidence away and commented, "If any of you have thoughts on who would try to incriminate your friend and teacher, give me a call. This . . ." He lifted the evidence. "Makes her look guilty."

A gasp rounded the room, gathering into a loud refusal to believe I could commit a crime. I held my breath for fear Kilbride would mention Ohio and reveal my secret, but he kept the news to himself.

I stepped forward so I stood next to the tall brute and eyed everyone as they settled at their seats.

"Thanks for sharing with Detective Kilbride. I'm sure he appreciates your help." I gave Kilbride a slight nod toward the exit.

He left, and I turned to the group. When all eyes remained on me, I stopped in my tracks.

"Katie has a crush on the cop," Gretchen teased.

I responded in a snap. "No, Katie thinks the detective is a pain in her side." I smiled to dull the thrust of the words before I asked who wanted tea.

With their overwhelming and favorable response, I set the kettle to boil and passed out cups along with the tea bag container. I brought forth a box of cookies from under the cash register and tossed it to Bill.

Before our break ended, we discussed the forthcoming show and decided on the set-up schedule.

I suggested the day prior to the opening would be ideal.

That way, should there be a need for last minute changes, I'd have a chance to address them.

"I can arrive early if you need me, Katie," Bill offered.

The ringing phone interrupted us. I excused myself and took the call while the others chatted on.

"Hey Katie, this is Ray Jenkins at the newspaper. Do you have time for an interview today?"

"About what?" My speck of inner peace shattered in an instant. Of course Ray would want an exclusive on Flora's death. Why the media hadn't already shown up could only mean the situation wasn't newsworthy, nationally or statewide. Alarm threaded along my nerves as I tried to think of a reason to avoid him. In the end, I agreed to see him at his office around four o'clock.

"Thanks, Katie. I appreciate this."

I grimaced and said, "I'll see you then."

"Great, that's great." Excitement filled his voice.

If he wrote a good story about the murder, then he'd probably hit the viable journalist status he craved so badly. Truth be told, I dreaded the meeting.

The students left, I cleaned the room, and tucked away the notes they'd each made as reminders. Books, used for inspiration, lay strewn about a tabletop holding a magazine rack. I shuffled the pile together and stacked them neatly in the bookcase.

On a sigh, I headed into the kitchen for a late lunch with Jasmine. Some time alone was exactly what I needed to gather my thoughts, clear my mind, and regenerate my energy level.

Chapter 6

SHADOWS DEEPENED WITHIN the house as the sun hung low in the sky. I'd tangled a paper tile to relax and regroup before the interview I'd scheduled with Ray. With my confidence and energy renewed, I figured I could manage a simple interview. I lifted the three-and-a-half-inch square piece of watercolor paper, referred to as a tile. I admired the lines neatly tucked into one another. A gentle weighted ink dab where the weaves met each other became prominent after I'd pencil shaded along the edges and smudged the graphite with a blending stump. I set the petite rendering aside and prepared for Ray Jenkins' questions.

It was past four when I flicked the outer lights on. Moving from room to room, I clicked lamp switches. Rarely did I leave the house in darkness when I was away. Though the days were longer, night would already have fallen by the time I returned home.

Bundled in a heavy jacket, scarf, and gloves, I headed across the square. Dread marched alongside me, filling me with apprehension over the information Ray would request.

I'd reached the Schmitz Landing Daily Newspaper Office and hesitated at the door. Before I chickened out, I mumbled aloud, "Pull up your big girl panties and buck up, Katie." Then I entered the building.

The front desk was empty so I figured nobody was left to man it. I called Ray's name and heard him yell for me to come back to his office. This, my first visit, left me wondering how and where I'd find him in this cavernous tomb. High ceilings, brick walls, antiquated desks, and no people to show me the way, left me jittery at best.

I wandered down a hallway before I called out again. Ray poked his head around a door casing and grinned. His freckled face beamed with excitement. His red hair stood on end as though he'd run his hands through it numerous times. I chuckled because I tended to do the same thing when working out an issue with a painting.

"Good to see you, Katie. Come in, come in." He took my arm and pulled me into his office.

He hauled a chair close to the desk where his laptop sat open and ready. My pulse rate hiked and my mouth was parched like a desert. I sucked in enough air that I thought my lungs would burst.

He asked question after question, worse than the ones Jonah Kilbride had battered me with. I didn't have any information to share other than having found Flora.

Exasperated, Ray's freckled face turned red and deepened to burgundy. Alarmed, I stilled. Then I reached out and touched his arm. "Are you all right, Ray?"

In his loud voice, he said, "Fine, I'm fine. I have to get this story out and it means everything to me to be the first paper to run with it. You understand, right, Katie?"

"I guess, but upsetting yourself isn't healthy, Ray. Relax. You'll get your story, I'm sure of it. Have you spoken with Detective Kilbride yet?"

"He's been unavailable for comment." Ray peered at me and then smiled.

I didn't care for the smile. It left me wary.

Ray asked, "Has Kilbride interviewed you?"

I nodded. "And he dropped by and questioned the students." Wishing I'd kept that to myself, I sat back in the chair and tried not to fidget.

"Why did he talk to the students?"

Now, sure that Ray could smell a story a mile off, I remained momentarily quiet. He'd jumped on my words the minute they left my mouth. *Crap.*

I told him a half-truth and hoped he couldn't tell. "I'm not sure what he wanted. He asked for theories concerning Flora's enemies."

Ray's keen brown eyes searched my face. "What were their responses?" His fingers tapped the computer keys.

I hesitated for a second and then shrugged. "Everyone was reluctant to point their finger at any single person, so naturally, they were vague."

"Katie, you're not helping me much." He rose from his chair and slammed the laptop lid down. "If I can't break this murder story wide open and someone else gets the scoop before I do, then I can kiss this job good-bye." He ranted on. "Do you think I want to stay here in this puny town when I could work in New York of Chicago, maybe even Los Angeles?" He ran his hand through his hair.

The interview was obviously over. I left the chair, took my jacket and scarf, and readied to leave. I had my own issues to deal with and Ray's problems were the least of my worries.

At the moment, I topped Jonah's list of suspects. That, to me, was more important than a stupid newspaper article. Especially if Ray figured out I was front and center in Jonah's investigation.

"I understand your frustration, Ray, but I can't give you information I don't have. Please, continue to try to contact Detective Kilbride. He should have the answers you seek." I smiled and hurried from the office, making my way along the corridor. Once I'd left the newspaper offices behind, I headed for the cafe.

I'd just hung my coat on a rack near the entrance and sidled onto a stool when Janet strode forward with a coffee mug and a steaming pot of brew. She greeted me with a cheerful grin and filled the cup.

"I saw you rush from the *Daily*. What's up, Katie?" Her eyes twinkled with humor and she giggled as I scalded my mouth on the hottest coffee I'd ever gulped. "*Ouch!*"

Instead of leaving to bring me cold water, she tossed a

sugar packet in my direction and told me to spread it inside my mouth to relieve the burn. Mystified by her advice, I ripped the corner off, emptied the white granules over my tongue and rubbed the substance around my gums. The pain ceased, the burn disappeared, and I looked at Janet in awe.

"You are so smart. I'd never have thought of that. Don't tell me ... It's an old family trick, isn't it?"

She laughed and nodded. "What else can I get you besides coffee?"

"I'd like the zurgischnatzlets and rosti special listed on the wall menu."

I sipped the coffee and waited to be served. The thought of zurgischnatzlets — a tasty dish of thin veal strips and mushrooms in a cream sauce, nestled alongside rosti, fried shredded potatoes similar to American shredded potato cakes — had my mouth watering in anticipation of the tasty fare.

A cold puff of air chilled my back when the door opened. I glanced back. Jonah tossed his jacket on the rack and walked toward the empty stool next to mine. His expression was tight and his eyes held a look I'd come to dread. I sighed and waited for his pearls of wisdom to tumble forth.

My meal arrived, heaped on the dish. Creamy sauce huddled over veal strips and trickled toward the rosti. I dug in with fervor. To heck with pearls of wisdom, I'd come to eat and nothing could stop me.

"You should know by now how to keep your trap shut, Ms. Greer." His soft-spoken words reached my ears as I chewed.

Around a mouthful of potato, I asked, "What's picking at you now, Kilbride?"

"Ray Jenkins called my office fifteen times today. His latest message said you highly recommended I speak to him concerning Flora Middly's murder investigation." He slanted his cold eyes in my direction. "Now why would he be bold enough to involve your name in his request?"

"Got me there. No clue." I chomped mushrooms and gulped coffee. Janet refilled the mug and took Jonah's order before she walked away.

"Ms. Greer, I dislike it when people lie to me. You're lying now, and have lied to me before. Now, I'll ask again, why did Jenkins involve you in his message to me?"

"He might have thought my name would urge you to cooperate with him," I answered. "I don't know how things worked in New York City, but I bet folks around here want word on your progress."

His stare was dangerous and frigid when he whispered, "Shall I tell them you top my suspect list? Should I share your past with Ray, Katarina?"

"Don't call me that," I snapped. "And threats don't suit you. You'd do well to remember I'm not easily intimidated, Kilbride."

I placed the cost of the meal and a tip for Janet next to the check and rose from the stool.

"See ya, Kilbride." I waved good-bye to Janet. Kilbride's snort at my arrogance filtered after me as I slipped into my jacket and tied the scarf around my collar. My temper was hot, and Jonah's threat to expose my past pricked my nerve endings … set them on fire.

I walked the park twice and formed a plan.

Chapter 7

ONE RING ... Two. Three. Crystal answered on the fourth. I let out a sigh of relief that she hadn't moved to Hawaii — I knew she'd been joking.

"Crystal Montague." Her strong, Georgia accented voice filtered over the phone line.

"Hi Crystal, it's me."

She barked, "Where the hell are you? I haven't heard a word from you in nearly a year."

"I moved to Schmitz Landing, New Hampshire. My name is now Katie Greer."

"Your legal name or an also-known-as?" Crystal snapped.

"Either way, Katarina Granger no longer exists."

Crystal laughed, a soul-chilling sound at the best of times.

"I'll hand it to you, girl. You've got balls. Now, what can I do for you? You haven't been arrested again, have you? I'm licensed for New Hampshire, though I don't have time to go out there at the moment."

After a few interruptions, I managed to fill Crystal in on my life for the past couple of days and explained Flora's Middly's consistent meddling and subsequent murder.

"Girl, can't you stay out of the limelight for one freakin' minute?" she asked, her drawl flavoring every syllable.

I smiled. Crystal took no prisoners and didn't suffer fools either. In the past, I'd called-in a favor from my father's friend at the Ohio Court of Appeals when my arrest appeared imminent. Judge Frame recommended Crystal as the sharpest, toughest lawyer he'd ever met and he'd been oh, so correct on that score.

"Look, I didn't kill Flora. Detective Kilbride has snooped into my past. He knows my background, most of it anyway, and has threatened to go public. We aren't close friends. Understand what I'm saying?"

"What's his name again?"

I told her and added he was from the Big Apple. I also mentioned he'd left the NYPD, and told her about his secretive attitude when I'd bugged him about that.

"Have you thought to tread gently on his toes? It isn't smart to charge ahead without knowing your destination, Kat. I have a friend who works for the attorney general's office in New York City. I'll ask him look into this cop's record. When I have news, you'll hear from me. In the meantime, stay the hell out of trouble and don't provoke this man. Understand me, here?"

"Gotcha, I'll refrain from an all-out war until I hear from you. I forgot how much I used to look forward to our conversations." I laughed and disconnected the call.

Three hours later, the phone rang. I listened, took notes, and agreed to be careful. Crystal said she'd call again if she could gather additional dirt on Kilbride. I thanked her, told her to bill me, and listened as she roared with laughter and said she would.

The words I'd scrawled across the pad, jumped out at me. I knew his secret, or so I thought. I'd leveled the dance floor and could now take the lead. I smirked at the image of Jonah's face should he ever again threaten me with exposure.

The evening hours were long past when I yawned, lifted Jasmine off the arm of the chair where she'd been napping, and decided it was time to turn in. I was switching off lights throughout the house and on the grounds when Jonah's cruiser stopped out front. I waited to see if he'd come to arrest me.

His long strides brought him up the steps and onto the porch before I blinked. Crap. He gestured for me to open up. I glanced at my watch.

Jonah waggled a finger at me and gestured again. I groaned and stood aside as he walked in.

"Why didn't you call first before coming over? I was about

to call it a night."

"Listen Ms. Crankypants, I wanted to apologize for my behavior at the cafe. Don't make me take the apology back. I was out of line, and I shouldn't have threatened you. I'm sorry."

Taken aback, I stood there dumbfounded. With a nod, I accepted his words of remorse. I didn't expect his amends would last long once we began to circle one another as was the case when he poked his nose where it didn't belong.

"Now, can we be friends?" he asked.

Yeah, like that would ever happen. Hesitant, I agreed to be friendlier and to show more cooperation.

"Thank you for the apology." Some things are just too good to be real, and this was one of those. I didn't believe he wanted to atone for his behavior, not for a minute.

He walked into the night with a smile on his face as though he'd just won the lottery. I waited until the car pulled away from the curb, then locked up, set the alarm, and shut down for the night.

With Jasmine tucked under my arm, I climbed the staircase. From under the heavy quilted coverlet, I listened to her purr. I must have drifted off, because I awoke later with a start. Sweat soaked my hair. My eyes were wide open and I caught the scream before it left my throat.

The dream lay bright and bold in my mind. I sat up, stuffed a pillow behind me, and remembered.

I stepped into the parlor. My father lay in a bloody heap on the floor a few feet from my mother. As I rushed toward them, strong fingers dug deep into the flesh of my arm. I slammed hard against a muscular body. I struggled, fearful and intent on escape, when the sharp blade grazed my collarbone and sank into the skin of my shoulder, then my arm, and into the left side of my body. I screamed, soundlessly in my dream, and fought until so much blood oozed that I weakened.

I peered inward, in search of the one thing that niggled at the back of my mind. This time I saw that a tattoo snaked around his hand, up his arm, and onto the muscled shoulder of my would-be killer. I stared without seeing as his face took shape.

Oh, God! It was *him*. I knew the killer.

The phone on the nightstand blinked as I picked it off the charger. Crystal's number rang and rang until I almost hung up.

In a sleepy voice my lawyer mumbled, "This better be good or your ass is in a world of shit."

I couldn't help but grin, even though I was shocked at the revelation I had to share with her. Crystal could turn even the most stressing event into a manageable situation. It must have been a gift at birth, because I knew no other person with her ability.

"I remembered something."

She yawned and sighed. "And this couldn't wait until morning, Kat?"

"No. *The dream* has visited me quite often lately. I couldn't ever recall it in detail until tonight. I know who killed my parents and attacked me. And, you're not gonna like it."

"Well, honey," she crooned, "just tell me and get it over with. I'm listening."

I breathed hard, unable to believe who the attacker was. "Jeremy Bronson did it."

The silence lasted so long I thought I had been disconnected. I shook the phone and said, "Are you still there?"

"I am." She didn't say another word for a short span of time until she said, "I'll take that news to Detective Brent. You know he's going to want to speak with you, right?"

"I know. I'm not about to return to Ohio and you can tell him I said so. You handle the wonder of blunders. He's nothing but a jerk anyway."

"I'll stay in touch, Kat. What you've just told me could be false, right?"

"No, I don't think so. The images came to me as bright as day. It's never happened before. Look into his whereabouts and I'll await your call. Good night, Crystal." Before she could respond, I cradled the phone.

The one person in the world I'd never considered as the

murderer was Jeremy Bronson. Where had he been all this time? The day we parted ways should have told me I hadn't seen the last of him. I hadn't put it all together ... I was too innocent back then — unlike what I was now.

That June was such a fresh and sweet-smelling month. My family and I had lived in an upscale neighborhood on the outskirts of Columbus, Ohio. I'd recently returned from a Chicago gallery show that had my art displayed front and center. The critics had wined and dined me. Photos of the opening had played in the news and online. Excitement filled the air, leaving me vibrant and enthusiastic about life. My work went viral before I realized it and sales skyrocketed beyond my wildest imaginings. High on life, I returned home to find Jeremy waiting on the doorstep.

He said he planned to return to Jersey. Surprised at the news, since I'd thought we were in a serious relationship, I asked why. It seemed his lifestyle didn't include a woman, namely me, with stars in her eyes and who had no plans for a family or husband.

He'd tossed a newspaper at me. A picture of me wrapped in the arms of a rock star that attended the opening — who'd taken advantage of the chance for publicity — filled the front page of the art section. Astounded by his attitude and revelation, I tried to explain it was nothing more than a stunt on the publicist's part.

Jeremy would have none of it. His words had cut deep, and now I knew his knife had as well. Jealousy ... there's nothing good about it.

That was the last time I remembered seeing Jeremy.

He'd climbed onto his motorcycle and driven away without any care for me — or so I'd thought. Now I knew that a month later, he had entered my parents' home, struggled with my mother and father, and killed them both before I interrupted his burglary of my father's famous painting collection.

Several hours, three cups of the strongest coffee I could make, and five tangled tiles later, the studio phone rang. The sun peeked over the horizon as I answered the call.

"You're sure you've remembered your parents' murderer correctly?" Detective Franklin Brent's gravelly voice sounded in my ear.

"Good morning to you, too, Detective Brent." I summoned the strength I'd need to deal with this interrogator extraordinaire. Mean, brawny, and shrewd, he was the best cop in Columbus ... Everyone said so. I thought of him as a cop with an attitude the size of Texas, who figured he was always right, and I never made the mistake of thinking otherwise. He'd been wrong about me and that just annoyed the snot right out of him.

"Answer the question," he demanded.

"Yes, I have. Do you know where he's been since my parents died?"

"I'm tracing him as we speak. I wanted to make sure you're positive before I begin a chase. You threw me under the bus the last time we met. I don't want that to happen again, you hear me? This isn't a game we're playing."

My temper rose. "If it had been a real bus, we wouldn't be having this conversation. I didn't consider it a game then, and I don't look at things that way now. Get over yourself, Brent. I'm sure Jeremy Bronson is the man you refused to look for." I smirked and said, "And doesn't the fact that I've finally remembered annoy you just a tad?"

I heard a heavy grunt and then he growled, "You better be right or you'll be thrown under the bus this time." The line went dead.

I'd already set the phone on the charger when it rang again. I sucked in some air and said, "Hello."

"Jeremy Bronson is being sought as we speak, Kat," Crystal assured me.

"Yeah, wonder of all wonders. Brent just called me. He's still steaming over the fact he was wrong."

"Glad he followed up with you. He'll possibly call Detective what's-his-name ... uh, Kilbride, too, so watch out for yourself, you hear me? I can't protect from here."

"I know that. I can take care of myself. Stay tuned, okay?"

Her haunting laugh chilled me as we disconnected. I sensed my life was about to become hellish. I left the studio table and headed to the kitchen for breakfast and more coffee. It was going to be a long day at Tangled Wings Studio.

Chapter 8

THE THIRD CALL of the morning came around eight o'clock. Jasmine crunched cat snacks while I finished dressing. The call came from reporter, Ray Jenkins. His voice sounded distant and strange. He asked if I could run over before class. He had something he wanted to discuss and couldn't explain over the phone. Reluctant to experience another of his outbursts, I agreed but said I couldn't stay long since I had to open for class at nine.

Wrapped for winter, I scooted across the park, crossed the busy street, and entered the newspaper building. The front desk sat empty and the eeriness of the building caught me unawares again. Ray must have come to work early since nobody else seemed to have arrived.

I sauntered through the hallway to his office. He lay inert on the floor. The gash on his head seeped blood. I stepped past him and called the police. While I waited, I peered at Jenkins and then kneeled beside him. Apprehension filled my every molecule.

Sirens blared, followed by the pounding of feet that thudded over the hardwood flooring. Kilbride called out and I answered. I glanced over my shoulder. He rounded the corner and stopped short a few feet away.

In my own defense, and to let Kilbride know Ray wasn't dead, I said, "He's breathing. I don't know what happened."

His face stern, Kilbride barked an order. "Move aside, Katie. Don't touch him, or anything else."

This time, I followed his direction. I observed the manner in which Kilbride treated Ray and the immediate area surrounding him. He gently shook the reporter, asking if Ray could hear him.

A slight moan emanated from Ray's throat, but he didn't open his eyes. Impatient, the rescue team waited for Kilbride's okay before approaching the victim.

Lead rescuer, Jim Haggerty, stepped forward. He gave me a nod and addressed Kilbride in a soft voice, asking about Ray.

Moving aside, Kilbride allowed Jim the opportunity to inspect Ray's injury. I remained silent, but had backed up against the nearest wall. The team immobilized Ray's neck and head before they loaded him onto the stretcher and rolled him to their awaiting truck. I followed at a snail's pace, wondering what would happen next.

Kilbride rounded on me, wrapped his strong fingers around my arm, and hurried me through the hallway to the front desk. He leaned against it with his arms folded.

"What the hell are you doing here?" His harsh voice boomed off the bricks.

"I received a call from Ray about twenty minutes ago. He asked me to come over. I found him like that upon arrival. I know nothing else. Honest."

He studied my face before he decided I hadn't lied. He glanced around the office and told me to go home, that he'd stop by later.

The ominous tone of his voice clearly said he was serious. "Be there after class has ended, Katarina, or you'll be sorry. You have questions to answer, and I won't brook any lies this time. Understand?"

"Got it. Yup, I'll be there," I said, and sidled from the building. If my trip home had been the Indy 500, I'd have won hands down. I crossed the park and entered the studio as if the devil were at my heels.

I rushed in, slammed the door, swore a few times, and ranted like a maniac on amphetamines. Could my life get any worse? Yeah, if I got arrested, my internal voice reminded me.

Upset, I marched to and fro until I'd managed to relieve

some of my anger over events of the past days.

I'd just entered the studio when the group of students charged inside. They all asked questions at once. The din of their voices was garbled at best. I put my hands up and requested everyone calm themselves.

"We have lots of work to do before the gallery opening. Let's settle in. Then I'll answer your questions and you can get started."

Jasmine perched on the cash register, eyeing each individual in turn. She jumped to the table, allowed her coat to be stroked by all, and then left the room at a sedate pace.

A slight chuckle followed her. Francine smiled and Freda shuffled her tiles like playing cards.

"That cat of yours is lovely and soothing, Katie," Francine said while she laid her tiles on the table before her.

"She is at that. Now ask what you will," I commented with a quick glance around the room.

The crew was interested in what happened at the *Daily*. Gretchen said she'd seen me rush across the park like I was being chased. Brenna noticed me going into the newspaper office as she entered the cafe for coffee before class began. Janet hadn't seen me, but saw the rescue fly down the street as she headed to the bakery. Bill knew nothing of the incident but was interested in hearing what I had to say. Freda was the only one who quietly waited in silence.

As my brief story ended, I mentioned Detective Kilbride would stop in later for a round of questions. Gretchen snickered, but said nothing. I slanted a look in her direction and ignored the inference that I looked forward to seeing him again.

The silence lay like a heavy blanket over the room. We proceeded with class. I smiled, knowing everyone had reached a yoga state of mind. I moved on soft-soled shoes, peeking at each tile, pleased at the effort behind each mark made. Brenna had reached the shading stage and gently slid the pencil tip along the edge of her lines. She glanced at me, smiled in a dreamy, relaxed manner, and began to blend the graphite with her blending stump.

The serene atmosphere was broken by Jasmine pawing at the front window. I glanced at her and then at the window. Jim Haggerty, lead rescuer, crooked a finger to summon me outside. I nodded, and told the class I'd return in a moment. I slipped Gretchen's handy coat over my shoulders.

The latch clicked softly as the door closed behind me. Jim leaned against the porch rail until I joined him.

"I've checked with the staff nurse. Ray's doing well. I thought you'd like to know, Katie."

We'd met at fundraisers for the fire company and at various events held in town. Tall and calm, Jim spent his days and nights rescuing cats, pets in general, and the people who lived in and visited Schmitz Landing. His reputation as a good man had been pointed out to me on more than one occasion. I smiled and thanked him for taking the time to stop by.

"You're having some bad luck right now, Katie. If there's anything I can do to help out, just say the word. In case you aren't aware of it, you've got a good rest and relaxation reputation among the residents in this town."

Unaware I'd become the poster woman for R&R in the area, I offered Jim a wide grin. "It's nice to know I'm not considered poorly. This week has been hard. I worry how gossip will affect business."

"No need, you're above reproach as far as the guys and I are concerned. We won't let you down. You've shown how much you care about the people here." He took the stairs in one downward stride and turned to say good-bye. He stared past me and I turned. Faces in the windows held grins, and speculation filled their eyes. Nothing nosey about my students … No sirree. I chuckled, waved Jim off, and returned to class as Kilbride's cruiser stopped at the gate. I guessed class time had come to an end.

The clock hand lined up at twelve when the students readied to leave and Gretchen took possession of her coat again. She leaned close and murmured, "What did Jim want?"

"He stopped by to say Ray is all right," I whispered.

"Jim's a fine man, Katie."

"So everyone keeps telling me. Gretch ... I'm not in the market for any man. They complicate life more than they're worth." I held the door open as she followed the others.

I waited for the thorn in my side to saunter inside at his leisure. He smiled at and greeted everyone, then turned to me. His face held a serious demeanor. Great.

"Jim Haggerty a friend of yours?" Kilbride wanted to know.

"That would be none of your business, Kilbride. Just state your business and then get out of my face." My mood had darkened at the prospect of yet another boxing match with this arrogant cop.

"Touchy, aren't we?" Kilbride smirked as he flipped through the pages of his worn notebook.

I glanced at the booklet and then slammed the studio door, hitched onto a stool, and propped my chin in my hand. I tried for a bored expression and must have achieved it since his eyes took on their usual frosty blue, angry look.

"Right, I spoke with Ray's co-workers this morning. I was told he's been anxious of late. Would you know why?"

Willing to cooperate to a point, I pondered the question. "He seemed upset yesterday when he interviewed me. It's important for him to get Flora's story out on the wire in order to be recognized as an investigative reporter. He feels this town is too small for him."

Kilbride's eyebrows hiked a notch. "He told you that?"

I nodded. "Yesterday, when we spoke, he raved about my unwillingness to be helpful and that you refused to give him something he could run with. Then he spouted off about wanting to move on to Chicago, New York, or some other metropolis where he'd become a major player. He was frustrated at the lack of cooperation compared to what he thought was due him."

Kilbride scribbled on his pad and then asked, "Why were you there today, and why so early?"

I sighed. Hadn't I made that clear earlier? Geesh!

"He called around eight this morning and insisted I come right over. I didn't want to since class started at nine, but he sounded strange and I figured I'd better go. When I arrived, he lay unconscious on the floor. Nobody was around and the building was creepy."

He measured my words before he asked, "You didn't hear or see anything else or anyone hanging about?"

"How many times and ways are you planning to ask me the same questions? I didn't see anyone, hear anything and, no, I didn't attack Ray. Cripes, Jonah, give me a break, will you?"

He changed tactics after he flipped a few pages in his little book. I'd give anything to see what he wrote in there.

"A Detective Brent called this morning. He wanted to give me a run down on your past. When I mentioned we were investigating a murder surrounding your shop, he wished me luck in a sarcastic tone. Why would he do that, Katarina?"

"I have asked you not to call me that. Are you deaf or just stupid?" I retorted.

He grinned, satisfied he'd gotten under my skin. What a smug jerk.

"So you have. I do like the name though and will use it whenever I want. Now, tell me about Detective Brent."

I lifted my shoulder in a half-shrug. "Nothing to tell. He's an egomaniac, and just like most cops, he thinks he's never wrong. He couldn't get the best of me, and had to concede defeat. You won't get far either."

"We'll see about that, Katarina. He tells me you've remembered your parents' murderer? Did that suddenly come out of the blue or what?" Disbelief filled his eyes, and the look on his face remained impersonal.

Why did he care? My memories had nothing to do with his case. Could he be on a fishing expedition? I offered him a narrowed stare and asked, "Why are my memories important to you?"

He roamed the room, glanced at various signs, prints, and tangles as he slowly paced. He swiveled a metal-backed chair, straddled it, and tossed the notebook down in front of him. His cell phone jingled.

He answered, listened, and then grunted before he pushed the end button.

"Rest assured Katarina, I will find out every detail about you should you try to impede this investigation. I won't tolerate the bullshit you handed Brent. He may be the top of his field in the cornfields of Ohio, but I'm a different type of investigator. Mark my words."

Ah, the threats begin. I took a giant step back in time as his harsh words hit home. Brent intimated more or less the same thing in those days. At first I'd been scared. I'd worked through my grief and worried over my lack of memory. Then Crystal entered my life. She'd taught me to watch what I said, how I said it, and to whom. She also educated me in the art of self-preservation.

"Idle threats, Kilbride. Idle threats." I tossed the words at him. "I know you have secrets, so you might want to think a bit before you resort to bullying to achieve your goals."

"What secrets?" His gaze held mine.

"For starters, how did that shooting really go down in the Big Apple, Kilbride?"

His movements swift, he gripped my arm before I could move away.

His teeth clenched, he uttered, "Don't play with me, Kat. You won't like the end game. Keep your mouth shut about New York." He gave me a slight shove when he let go.

Jasmine sat close, frozen in place by the tone of his voice. Her ears flattened back, claws exposed, she reached out and raked Kilbride's exposed hand.

Kilbride pulled his hand back, saw the blood slowly stain his skin where her claws had sunk in, and yelped. He glared at the cat and then at me.

"I guess she doesn't like your tone of voice any more than I do." I tossed him a tissue from my pocket and told him I'd get some peroxide for his mini-lacerations. I walked away satisfied that at least the cat would come to my defense.

Kilbride addressed his scratches, stopped the minor bleeding, and took his seat. Now that his anger was under control, he was silent while he watched Jasmine stalk back and forth between us.

"If you can keep a civil tongue in your mouth, and tone down your aggression, we can talk." I gave him a smug look. "If not, you'll deal with the cat."

He had the grace to agree, and then apologized to me over his rash behavior. He reached out to scratch Jasmine's ears. She turned away, sat at my elbow, and watched him.

Kilbride said, "I shouldn't have spoken to you that way. Sorry, what happened in New York, well, I try not to think about it. Besides that, Middly's death and now Jenkins' attack has the captain chewing me out on a regular basis. He wants this murder solved yesterday. He's says the town council is all over him because this is a tourist town."

Jasmine peered at Kilbride, her ears twitching. I smoothed her coat, calming her. She still didn't care for his tone of voice.

"Okay, okay, I get it," Kilbride said with a glimmer of mirth around the corners of his mouth. "She's ferocious."

"It's nice to have someone come to my rescue, even if it's Jasmine."

The feline turned in a circle and lay down in front of me, her purr loud and steady while I petted her.

"When Ray initially asked about Flora, I didn't want to discuss it. He's been nice to me since I moved here, so I agreed to speak with him. This morning he said he had something private to discuss and wouldn't talk on the phone. He insisted I meet him. I'm not sure what was on his mind, but he sounded mysterious."

Kilbride's phone rang again. When he answered, I noticed relief in his voice.

"He is? When? I'll be at the hospital shortly. Keep his room guarded. I don't want to take any chances. Understand?"

I leaned back in the chair. "Was that important?" I asked.

"Jenkins has fully regained consciousness. He's not hurt badly, but has one hell of a headache and possibly a concussion, from what I've been told." He fiddled with his pen after he thrust his notebook into his jacket pocket, and weighed his next words.

A sense of gloom weighed me down. I waited to see if he'd share his phone call, when he asked, "Want to take a ride?"

"Where?"

He stared at me for a second. "To see Ray Jenkins."

"Sure, why not? I could use some fresh air. I'll just get my coat."

Kilbride nodded when I agreed to join him. I returned through the hallway, swung my jacket on, and donned my gloves. Kilbride stood at the door.

He stared at Jasmine as she sauntered into the back of the house. "I have never seen a cat like that. She's quite a girl."

"She showed you who was boss, that's for sure. I found her half-starved near a dumpster outside the hotel where I'd stayed when I first arrived in town. She was sick, and I thought she'd likely die before I could bring her back to health. She's one tough cookie. Even the veterinarian was skeptical that she'd recover. The poor thing had such a serious case of pneumonia, suffered from starvation, and she was riddled with fleas that used her for an ongoing feast."

Kilbride parked close to the hospital entrance. The elevator stopped at the third floor and we were directed to Jenkins' room. An officer blocked Jenkins' doorway. He was obviously there to study staff and visitors who roamed the wide corridors.

Jonah nodded to him as the man stepped aside for us to enter the room. The cop was as rugged as Jonah, which begged the question of how many more were there like him?

The television screen flickered scenes with no sound. Jenkins' pale skin, shadowed eyes, and sutured head sent a shiver up my spine. I'd seen that type of thing before when I'd finally been allowed out of bed and into my hospital bathroom where I saw myself after the attack. My appearance had been ghastly. I'd been bandaged all over and looked like the walking dead.

Kilbride must have picked up on the tension I felt, because he gently drew me forward.

I stood at the bedside. "Ray, it's me, Katie," I murmured.

Ray's eyes flew open. It took a second for him to focus. I wondered if his vision was off kilter after the head trauma he'd received.

"Katie, Katie," he whispered and reached for my hand.

I gently clasped his hand and perched on a chair.

Offering him a slight smile, I asked, "What happened, Ray?"

"I don't really know. I waited for you, when suddenly it was lights-out. You didn't strike me, did you, Katie? How did I get here? Nobody wants to tell me anything."

When I was about to answer him, Jonah stepped forward. "Katie found you on the floor in front of your desk. You're lucky she did."

"Who did this to me? I don't remember." Ray's groggy, pain-filled voice faded. Apparently he felt as bad as he appeared and it was obvious the nurse had dosed him with drugs.

"We don't know what happened. I have yet to speak with the doctor concerning your injury," Jonah stated.

"Ray, is there anyone I can call for you?" I asked, withdrawing my hand and rising from the chair. Just the smell of the hospital left me edgy.

"The nurse has called my mother. She's on her way." He offered a weak smile. "Funny how we call Mom when something happens, huh?"

I stiffened at his words, and recovered as best I could. I patted his hand even though he'd subtly accused me of assault. "I hope you feel better soon, Ray." I followed Kilbride from the room.

Outside, Kilbride turned to me, a question in his eyes. Without a word, the officer on guard resumed his spot. He watched Kilbride and then gazed at me. I felt like a fly on a pin, unable to move, yet yearning to flee. Life really sucks sometimes.

Grasped by the arm, Kilbride ushered with me along the

hallway toward the nurses' station. He muttered something about sick cats and dangerous people as we moved. I couldn't understand all of it, but I was positive his words implied insult, where I was concerned. Call me paranoid, but that's the way it sounded.

I stopped and pulled my arm from his grasp. He, too, stopped and turned cold eyes to me.

I stepped close, standing on my toes to whisper in his ear. "What the hell do you think I've been doing?"

"Did you or did you not assault this man?" he asked, hands on his hips.

I quickly glanced around. People had started to gawk. I slid my hand into the crook of his elbow and nudged him to move while I offered a huge grin at those who watched.

"Get moving and don't make a scene, Kilbride," I mumbled. The door to my left held a placard with the word *Lounge* inscribed on it. I hustled the brute inside.

Once we were out of sight from inquisitive eyes, I rounded on Kilbride, full-on angry.

"What is this about? Did you bring me here to see how I would deal with Ray?"

He propped an elbow on the bookcase against the wall and shrugged. "Sort of. I wanted to see your reaction to his injury."

"Happy now? I detest hospitals as much as cops. If you're done with me, I'd like to go home. Now!" By this time, my anger was on fire. Anger had been phase one, and I'd moved to phase two, into full-blown temper mode. These flare-ups hadn't existed before my parents and I were filleted. My anger, concerning ill treatment by anyone, not just cops, welled and overflowed at times. It wasn't only the cat who could have an attitude.

I made for the door. "I'm leaving. Do whatever the hell you want." I tossed the words over my shoulder.

He hauled me back hard enough that my body slammed against his. "You think you can order me to take you home and just like that ..." He snapped his fingers. "I'll do as you say?

J.M. Griffin

We're not finished, yet Katie."

Breathless at our sudden contact, I stood momentarily surprised. In a snap, I shoved hard against his chest with both my palms and stumbled away from him. And he caught me. Pulled me back.

He glared with hot, sparkling eyes. He drew me closer to him, his mouth meeting mine in a searing kiss. A mind-numbing kiss, that is, if I'd had a mind left at all at that juncture.

The kiss seemed to last forever, but ended way too soon. When he released me, I took a deep breath, gazed into his fiery stare, and wondered how to deal with this overbearing, untrusting, police detective I'd become attracted to. What was I thinking, to allow that?

"Are we done?" I asked.

Kilbride backed off, his face a mask of dislike.

"For now," he said softly. "I'll take you home."

Chapter 9

THE UNSETTLING, SILENT ride frayed my jangled nerves. At this rate, I wouldn't have any common sense left. I sighed, gazed out the passenger window, and tried to think about the good things I'd come to expect.

My studio, the cat, my new life. Those were what made me happy. Why I was in the midst of a mystery, could only be attributed to Flora Middly's miserable life — or lack thereof. I had nothing to do with it. I kept reiterating those words, over and over until it became my mantra.

We stopped at the front gate. Kilbride walked around to the passenger door, opened it, and waited for me to step onto the sidewalk. He casually observed the neighborhood.

There was little traffic and no nightlife to speak of. The odd person entered the public library across the square. People who gathered at the Swiss Café for a coffee and conversation were the only foot traffic about. Stores closed down early in winter. Gift shops shuttered at seven o'clock. The market, pharmacy, and the like, remained open later, but not by much.

"I'll walk you to the door," Kilbride stated in a flat voice.

"Fine," I said, still in a huff about what he'd said at the hospital.

He cast a sideways glance at me. I stepped quickly in his wake as he strode to the house.

Jonah left me at the porch steps. I watched him walk to the car, where he turned to peer at my house before he drove off.

I leaned against the wall, and hefted a sigh the size of Texas. My sweet lifestyle had abruptly ended. The murder and the attack on Ray could ruin my business and everything I had worked so hard for.

Once the lock clicked in place, I set the alarm and wandered toward the cozy area of the house. I'd left the fireplace set on low. Soft light glowed from the small reading lamp, and Jasmine lay curled in a ball on the settee. I smiled wearily and flounced onto the chair.

I hadn't made any enemies since I'd settled in Schmitz Landing — other than Flora.

How had things fallen out of balance? How had they gone so horribly wrong in such a short time?

And if Jonah believed I was guilty, why had he kissed me?

The questions bounced around inside my head. I had no answers ... no acceptable answers, anyway.

I poured a glass of wine, slouched in the chair again, and took out a pad of paper and a pencil. I wrote the questions that bothered me. Then I wrote my answers. When I looked at what I'd written on the paper, goose bumps formed on my arms. I shook my head and refused to believe what I'd scribbled on the page. It didn't make sense. I needed more information about several of the town residents.

It concerned me to think I was Jonah's number one suspect.

When the phone rang, I swept it off the charger.

Gretchen's voice echoed in my ear.

"Did you visit Ray?"

"Yeah, he has a concussion," I answered. "Detective Kilbride took me to see him. He thought I might have knocked Ray out. Before you ask, I have no clue why, so don't bother."

"He took you to see Ray? He accused you? What a jerk."

"Ray's going to be fine. His mother was on her way to the hospital and the good detective dropped me here at home."

"I can't believe Kilbride suspects you of such a thing ..."

I chuckled at her indignant words. "He's doing his job. Since I found Ray and was there when Kilbride arrived, I suppose I look guilty. I also think this Flora thing has him troubled."

Gretchen made a few more ungracious remarks before

she hung up with the promise she'd see me the next day. I said good-bye and disconnected the call.

I awoke with a start, the blankets tossed to the floor in a jumbled mess. The cat stared from the bottom of the bed, her ears flattened back, and her eyes narrowed.

I lay back against the pillows trying to figure out what had awoken me and I must have dozed again, because I jumped when the alarm clock blared.

After some deep breaths, I shook my hands, and began a yoga routine. In a better frame of mind, I showered and dressed, promising to treat myself to a tangle to help me stay relaxed. After all, isn't that what I taught others to do when they were overwhelmed with anxiety and stress?

Jasmine joined me at the top of the stairs and we scooted down together.

I had straightened the house, gulped down two cups of coffee, and eaten breakfast, before I headed into the gallery. I considered general space issues while I studied the room with its stunning beveled glass windows. My daily group came up the sidewalk.

As they made their way toward the studio, I went to greet them. They jostled each other to get out of the chilly air.

With their usual cheerfulness, they went straight to work. The opening was in two days' time and each student had tangles to finish. I left them to it and wandered back into the gallery.

Bill stuck his head around the corner. "Can I be of help, Katie?"

"Sure. While I bring pieces downstairs from my storage area you can move those pieces of furniture closer together." I pointed at a couple chairs.

With a nod, Bill began to shuffle the chairs about.

I returned with a stack of framed tangles, some large, some small — all of them wonderful.

"I could use a hand hanging these."

Bill rushed to assist with the heavier frames. A few odd pieces of furniture, decorated by Janet and Gretchen, would be brought in later. Freda and Francine only worked on paper. Bill tried his hand at paper, porcelain, and glass.

The various pieces of work were all breathtaking, in their own way. No doubt the show would be a success. The last one I'd held consisted of my own work and not that of students.

Sometime later, the tea kettle whistled. I glanced at Bill and summoned him to follow me. He wiped the sweat from his brow, and murmured something about needing a break. Laughingly, he stated I was a 'slave driver.'

We found tea mugs, filled and waiting on the table. I gazed at the tangles laid out before me and smiled.

"This is all wonderful work. I'm so pleased by your efforts," I exclaimed with pride.

Excitement shone in their eyes as I expressed my opinions of each work for display.

"You've all done such a great job. I just know this show will be successful." I glanced around and continued. "Bill and I have hung some of the framed work if you'd like to take a look."

The words were hardly out of my mouth when Freda led the way into the gallery. Sounds of awe echoed off the walls as each student gazed at the artwork.

Freda grinned with pleasure and said, "We've outdone ourselves." She turned toward me. "You always said tangles should be put away for a while once they're finished and then looked at later. Now I understand. I *do* see it with new eyes. You're so right, Katie."

Francine waved her hands with enthusiasm while she praised each and every artwork. Her high energy brought a round of smiles and agreement from the group.

"Can we help you set up any of the other pieces you stored for us?" Janet asked.

I nodded, and directed all but Freda to the storage area. It didn't take long to bring the remaining pieces downstairs. Freda, with barely concealed excitement, remarked on all that was hung and placed about the room. She redirected the positioning of some of the art, insisting it be shown at its best. I chuckled at the excitement exuding from the group.

The remainder of our time passed. Bill glanced at his watch, remarked that class was over, and that the others should be on their way to their respective jobs and whatnot.

With a grin, I waved them out the door with a promise they'd see me the next day.

Coffee and pie at the Swiss Café would be my treat after I'd finished in the studio. I stared at the pieces of art from different angles and figured we were ready for Friday's opening.

I grabbed my jacket and scarf, and headed out the door with my wallet and house keys in my pocket. The café lay opposite the Town Center. Crossing the snow-covered green, I admired the scrolled benches set along the path overshadowed by elm trees.

Once inside, I took a stool at the counter. Janet waved from the other end of the room. Holding up her index finger, she signaled she'd be with me in a minute. I nodded and read a menu.

Three people from the Wellness Center caught my attention when I glanced up. They stared at me, turned away, and began to whisper among themselves. It was then that I thought I'd become more than Jonah's chief suspect. I had also become the gossip of Schmitz Landing.

When they looked up again, I smiled and waved. It would be easy to take offense, but I refused to allow paranoia to ruin the day. I might not even be their topic of conversation.

Janet set a large slab of the apple pie I'd ordered in front of me. She filled my cup with coffee whenever it looked low. I smiled, relishing the attention. Just as she leaned forward, one of the wellness groupies tapped me on the shoulder.

Hannah Stone gestured to the others who made ready to leave, and said, "We wondered if you would teach another tangle class at the center, Katie? The last one was so relaxing there's been another request for it. What do you say?"

Stunned, I smiled and agreed to hold a class after this show had come and gone. *So much for paranoia.* Hannah beckoned to the others and with a thumbs up, declared the class was on.

Excited over the prospect of a class, they promised to bring friends and relatives.

Having been asked to teach a new and different group to tangle, and where I could explain its benefits, brightened my day. My present students were fun, but all teachers hope to widen their student base and share their talent. I'm no different. I ordered another slice of pie to go and sipped the last of my coffee when a rush of cold air chilled me.

I glanced over my shoulder. Jonah Kilbride was hanging up his jacket. The impulse to leave left when I considered how foolish that idea was. Why should I scurry away? Maybe because we'd had that hot, long-lasting, not-long-enough kiss at the hospital. The one I wasn't sure what to think of.

I'd shied away from considering what that kiss meant. Could I trust a man of the law? Did he want a relationship or had I simply annoyed him enough to kiss me? Questions like these would have to wait because the man in question slid onto the empty seat next to me.

"Hey Katie, how's the pie?"

I said it was delicious. Nothing more than a simple answer. I chewed the pie thoughtfully, considering what might be in store for me next. My excitement of the last few minutes fled as my day suddenly turned gray.

Without another word, Jonah dug into the pie Janet brought him. He picked the last crumbs from the plate with his fork and savored the taste. I couldn't help but smirk over his enjoyment.

"What brings you to the diner, Kilbride?"

Jonah's gaze lingered on my mouth as the corners of his eyes crinkled. He smiled. "The dessert, of course. Isn't that why you're here?"

"Absolutely." Wary, I picked up the wrapped piece of pie and slid off the stool, using the excuse I had an appointment. I fastened my jacket, and pulled my gloves from the pockets. I placed money on the counter to cover the bill and tip.

Janet stood at the register, a curious expression on her face. She gave me a wink and a knowing grin. I pointed to the cash and bid Jonah farewell.

"I'm leaving, too. Can I give you a lift?" Jonah offered.

"No thanks, I'm not going far." I scooted from the building.

The clear sidewalk made for easy travel. I tried not to hurry and regarded window dressings of shops I passed. The Wellness Center sat at the street corner.

The secretary and owner greeted me with warmth and cheer. Penny's happiness was contagious. Her energy and positive sense of wellbeing emanated throughout the room. I figured I should come here for some improved wellness of my own. Whether it would be in the form of a single or group yoga class, I determined that my situation warranted a treat.

Penny Prince, a slight woman of thirty-something years, ran the center. Her ballet dancer poise and grace complemented her shoulder-length hair, tied ponytail style. Sand-colored wisps had come loose and nestled along her forehead and sides of her face. Petite, she stood a bare five foot two.

Penny swept around the desk to give me a hug. Though I wasn't a hugger, I allowed the woman to give me one. I couldn't think of a way to avoid her obvious need to embrace everyone she knew. Her long thin fingers, on fine delicate hands, gripped me with unexpected strength. Laughing, I stepped from her grasp.

"It's good to see you," I remarked while I removed my outer winter wear. "How've you been?"

"Fine, fine. Though I've wondered how you've been coping after you found Flora. And, if that wasn't bad enough, I heard Ray Jenkins had an accident. Geez, Katie, you need to come here to unwind." She chuckled and hung my garments on a nearby coat stand.

"What brings you by?" Penny asked as she turned.

"Hannah Stone requested another Zentangle class here at the center. Were you aware the group wanted one?"

Penny nodded and said, "I was supposed to contact you

earlier this week, but my mother isn't well, so I didn't make the call. I'm sorry about that. When would you like to come in?"

"How about the end of next week? I want the gallery opening out of the way first." I checked the huge calendar of events posted on the wall.

"Then next week it is. I'll call the newspaper and get that on the advertising schedule once you select a day and time."

I studied the calendar and my schedule, then set the class and explained the program I had in mind. Always amenable, Penny agreed and marked the calendar accordingly. She stood back and summed me up in one quick skim.

Penny sighed. "If you don't mind my saying so, you look a little out of sorts. Are you sleeping well?"

I groaned. "As a matter of fact, I'm not. This whole Flora affair, coupled with Ray's incident, has caused me some unrest. I should register for your yoga sessions. Tangling has helped, but I think something more would be a plus."

"Then let's get you started." Penny pulled her roster off the desk. She mentioned the days and evenings with openings. I registered to attend a class held early in the evening three times a week.

The arrangements made, I left the center and shopped the nearest clothing store for leotards to wear to the classes. My usual exercise clothing consisted of sweatpants.

As I left the shop, I heard my name called from a distance. I turned toward the sound. Jonah hurried along the block to catch up.

When he arrived, he said, "I wanted to let you know that Ray is out of the hospital. He'll return to work tomorrow. He said he slipped and fell at the office."

Silent for a second, I asked, "So, this is your way of telling me you're sorry for accusing me of conking him on the head?"

He'd been smiling, but that wonderful sight faded as I spoke. Jonah shook his head, his lips tightened, his eyes chilled.

Watching his face change from happy to angry and disappointed, I figured my assumption was wrong.

He snapped, "That's not what I meant and you know it. I wanted to tell you he was fine and that he remembered what happened." Jonah briefly glanced around the street before he said, "Next time I won't bother."

"Let's hope there won't be a next time, Kilbride," I remarked and walked away, leaving him on the sidewalk. I huffed and puffed like a dragon as I marched across the village green. I'd taken quick offense and spoken abruptly to the man who ruffled my feathers and threw my life into chaos with a mere grin. Now I was disgusted with myself. I shrugged at the thought that he deserved better treatment. Maybe I'd make up for my rude behavior by adopting a better attitude toward him should he attend the opening ...

Chapter 10

GROUPS OF PEOPLE shuffled their feet in the brisk chill of the night, waiting to enter the gallery. Laughter and conversation drifted up the walk as I flung the door open and welcomed them inside. Jasmine made a beeline for the rear of the house and I closed the corridor door behind her.

With alacrity, I guided everyone into the gallery through the studio. I hung coats on hooks and laid many across work tables. The crowd kept coming. I wondered if the mishaps I'd been associated with were the reason for the number of attendees or if the ad had piqued their interest.

While class members chatted and showed their works, I handed out flyers and business cards. Sales soared, pieces were tagged with sold cards, and the students fairly beamed. Their excitement was palpable as I wandered the gallery chatting with visitors and answering questions concerning the benefits of tangling.

I waved to Penny, who entered with Hannah immediately after Jonah wandered in. Wearing a sweater and dress slacks, his attire enhanced the hardiness of Jonah's looks. My heart leapt as I fumbled with the flyers in my hand. His gaze brushed the crowd, locked onto me. The brochures fluttered to the floor.

Penny and Hannah made their way through the crowd, conversing with those they knew. Kneeling, I gathered the flyers and shuffled them together. A pair of feet stopped in front of me. I looked up, way up, into Jonah's humor-filled eyes. He reached down and took my arm as I rose.

"What a crowd. Your students must be happy," he said. He

glanced at the people who milled in front of the pictures, and smiled to acknowledge those who waved to him.

"They were lined up on the sidewalk quite early so I let them in. It's such brisk weather, I couldn't leave them out there to freeze."

"I see the wine is flowing well," Jonah observed.

"It's one way to loosen their tongues and their wallets. Sales are steady. I think we'll have a successful evening." I stepped to the side as Freda motioned to me.

"Excuse me, I think Freda is in need," I said as I stepped away.

Two men bickered as I stood behind them. Freda gave me a worried frown and tipped her head toward them.

One man declared, "You don't have to buy this. I know Freda did this piece for me. She as much as said so at church last Sunday."

The second man's face turned red. He blustered and asked Freda, "Is he telling the truth? Did you say this was for him?"

Before she could speak, I stepped between them. "I'm sure there's another of Freda's works that might suit either of you." I smiled and tucked my hand into the second man's arm, drawing him toward a detailed cart that stood against the wall.

"Freda mentioned she had a specific person in mind for this particular tea cart. I wondered who she had in mind and by gosh, I can see she must have been thinking of you."

He bought the line I tossed out and all but preened as he ran his hand over the lovely work covering the cart. While he perused it, I motioned to Gretchen. She promptly began a sales pitch that seemed to please the man more than I had. Either that, or the fact that Gretchen shamelessly poured on the charm concluded the sale.

I grinned, felt a warm breath on the nape of my neck, and listened to Jonah whisper to me.

"You know how to handle people, I'll give you that Katarina." He chuckled. "That man never knew what struck him, especially when Ms. Winters took over. The poor guy couldn't refuse the sale."

I turned, leaned into him, and said, "Why Jonah, are you here on business or is it simply pleasure?" I gave him a wink, smiled, and walked away before he could answer. I refused to become embroiled in what would likely end in an angry exchange.

Time seemed to fly. The hour grew late and scores of gawkers donned their coats while buyers paid for their purchases. I smiled until I thought my face would crack as thirty or so people said their good-byes.

Jonah lingered in front of Gretchen's illustration. Surrounded by Hannah, Gretchen, and Penny, he smiled affably and exuded a charisma that I hadn't yet witnessed. I wasn't the only one who could work a crowd.

With a shake of my head, I counted the sold cards tucked inside artwork and smiled at the number of sales made throughout the evening.

I tallied the receipts from the register. Bill sold all his work, Gretchen had three of twelve pieces left, while Freda, Janet and Francine had sold all their framed art and some of their small furniture items. Walking toward the group, I heartily congratulated them for their sales. We laughed when Bill remarked he was exhausted and excited all at the same time.

"I may not sleep tonight, just thinkin' of the huge gathering and how many of them bought our work."

Freda, who leaned heavily on her cane, asked if he'd take her home. With a nod, Bill raced from the room and returned with her long coat and matching hat. With his coat draped on his shoulders, he helped Freda with hers.

"Thank goodness there's nothing on my agenda tomorrow. I'm pooped," Freda remarked with a sparkle in her eyes as she headed out with Bill by her side.

Gretchen, Francine, and Janet cleared wine glasses and empty bottles from the library table beside the door. Gretchen marched along the corridor into my living quarters. Idle, Jonah waited until we were alone.

"Lucrative show," he commented. "Your students did well

and I bet you'll acquire more students from those brochures you handed out. Nice work."

Sincere though the compliment sounded, I was reluctant to take it at face value.

"Did you attend the opening to spy on me, or what?"

"Katarina, you are so suspicious. There's no reason why I can't enjoy art the same as everyone else, is there?" His face held a bland expression.

I glanced at the doorway to the corridor and hissed, "I've asked you not to call me that."

"So you have, and I've told you how much I like the name. I'll call you whatever I please." His grin tended toward a sneer, which left me to wonder what why he'd come and what would happen after the others truly left.

Glass smashed. I heard Jasmine's yowl and headed toward the noise. Her back was arched and my usually calm feline spit and growled as Gretchen, Francine, and Janet tried to soothe her. However, the closer they got, the wilder and more frenzied Jasmine became.

"Don't approach her. She won't allow you to pick her up," I warned the three of them. "I'll handle her. You should go back to the gallery. Thanks for cleaning up."

Each woman glanced at the other and left me to deal with my crazed feline. Soft voiced, I coaxed Jasmine from the corner. Her fur smoothed as I stroked her coat and the terrified look in her eyes dissipated once she cuddled within my arms.

His voice directly behind me, Jonah mentioned both of the females living in this house had attitudes to be wary of. I rounded on him and peered over the cat's shoulder.

"You should know." I smirked as he laughed.

"You're right. I'm well aware of your tendencies." He lifted the dustpan and broom dangling from a closet hook and swept up shards of broken glass. He dumped the debris and sauntered into the gallery.

"The girls have gone," he called. "They figured you're capable of handling Jasmine and the mess they made. Janet said they'll see you at the usual time on Monday."

Jasmine jumped from my arms and scooted upstairs. She hadn't acted this wild before tonight, and I assumed she was upset over the noise from the front rooms along with being locked out. Although, maybe she'd just been frightened by the sound of breaking glass.

With a sigh, I watched Jonah's casual actions and his smile when he returned from the gallery. What was he up to now? Curious, I waited to see what he planned and how he'd go about it.

He lightly wrapped his hand around my arm and led me into my cozy area where he pointed to my favorite chair. "Have a seat, I have a few questions, if you aren't too tired."

Crap and double crap. Couldn't I enjoy the rest of the evening without an interrogation? Would it be too much to ask?

"I'm sure it won't matter if I refuse, right?"

His soft laughter strummed at my heartstrings, even though I was certain he'd hammer at me until I couldn't stand it another minute. I refused to admit to something I didn't know or hadn't done. My backbone stiffened and I raised my eyes to his.

"You're determined to ruin the end of my evening, so go for it. I can't say how cooperative I'll be."

Again he smiled and stood before the fireplace. Cast in shadow, his appearance became foreboding. Suspicious, I caught my breath and waited. Every nerve in my body was wound like a taut violin string.

"Have you heard from the Ohio detective concerning the man sought for the murder of your parents?"

I sighed and picked at the fringe of the afghan covering the chair. "He hasn't called today. I guess they're still searching for Jeremy Bronson. Bronson seems to have left the planet."

"Maybe they aren't looking in the right place. People can disappear in big cities like New York, Chicago, and Los Angeles, or even in states like Montana, where you can hide in the wilderness without anyone aware that you're there. When the fear of being found fades, confidence and carelessness return. That's usually when mistakes are made and a criminal is caught."

He stared at me for a few moments, seated his long body in the chair opposite me, and appeared to relax. Far from relaxed myself, I could hear my heart pounding in my ears. *Was Jeremy here?* My chest tightened and suddenly I couldn't breathe. Was he a danger to me? Had he found me? Had I run away and changed my name for that reason ... or was it only because I wanted a new start? I'd actually written down that question when I'd begun to suspect things were about to run wild. I gasped for air. My throat seemed to close. The room darkened.

The next thing I knew, a cool, moist cloth was applied to my face. Soft words crooned their way into my head. I listened to Jonah's gentle summons to return to him. Was it my imagination? Did he want me for himself because he was romantically interested in me, or so he could arrest me for Flora's murder? I opened my eyes and stared at his rugged face, those concerned blue eyes, and luscious lips.

He leaned over me, kissed me softly, and said, "You darned near scared me to death."

"I must have passed out. I couldn't breathe and then darkness descended before I could move." I struggled to rise from the chair, but Jonah pushed me back and told me to be still until my body returned to normal.

For once, I listened and obeyed. Seconds later I felt better. Jonah left the room and returned with a splash of whiskey in a glass.

"Drink this fast. Don't hesitate."

"I'm not much of a whiskey drinker, but okay." The alcohol scorched my throat, warmed my stomach, and I coughed as the spirit awaked my innards. Dang that was strong stuff. I usually kept a bottle of whiskey on hand should Gretchen want something stronger than wine and I was glad of it now.

"Thanks," I said with a wheeze.

His laughter rounded the room and warmed my soul — the sound rich and deep in tone. I enjoyed Jonah's laugh.

He squatted in front of me and took my hands in his. He

held them while I relaxed.

"What brought that on?"

I hesitated to answer, but knew I'd have to explain. "After my parents died, I was in the hospital for some time. I'd had surgery after being rushed into the emergency room with heavy bleeding from wounds Jeremy inflicted on me — though I didn't know it was Jeremy at the time. Honestly, I don't know why I didn't die. When I was well enough to be on my own, my aunt arrived to help with my recovery."

I studied his hands, and the way he gently held mine. "I was told these anxiety attacks affected me in a similar way as soldiers who suffer from post traumatic stress react. Sudden shocking events, or unexpected surprises, such as what just happened here, result in angst that is sometimes difficult to deal with. I haven't had an attack in over a year. Sorry you had to witness that."

His face was unreadable, but his blue eyes showed his thoughts. Cold blue ice shards sparkled from their depths. Jonah's anger was easy to spot. Why was he angry? I didn't know, but assumed it might be over the fact I'd been viciously attacked. I understood then that his eyes would give him away before his facial expressions ever would. I stored that in the deep recesses of my mind for future reference.

He pulled a chair closer to mine and settled in. "If it's not too painful for you, tell me about life after your parents' deaths."

Leery of confiding in him, I fumbled with the afghan's fringe. "Why do you want to know?"

"I'd like to understand you better." He smiled. "And before you come back with a snarky attitude, Miss Crankypants, I don't believe for a moment that you killed Flora or attacked Ray."

I gazed at him for a while, weighing each of his words. He could find out from others what my life had been like after I left the hospital, so why not give him my unabridged version?

"The funeral was hell. I suffered an anxiety attack during the graveside ceremony. My aunt was smart enough to bring an ammonia inhalant and used it immediately to bring me around. I scared the bejeepers out of the mourners.

"After that I went through physical therapy and emotional therapy. Was told I'd blocked the incident from my mind as a protection device. My therapist wasn't concerned, but what the hell did he know? He hadn't seen his family sliced and diced." I ran a hand across my forehead and hauled in a huge breath.

"If it's too much for you, forget I asked," Jonah murmured.

"I've dealt with the destruction Jeremy caused, but I haven't had the chance to deal with him yet. I'm all right. Really, I am."

"If you say so, go ahead." Jonah's face remained alert and impersonal. He waited patiently while I gathered my thoughts.

"I returned home from hospital to find the house in perfect order. No blood, nothing to indicate there'd been a devastating murder. My parents might never have been killed if the way the house looked was any indication. It took some time before I could enter the room where I'd found them and where the assault on me took place.

"I got a few licks in before succumbing to his brutality. If the windows hadn't been open, our neighbor would never have heard the ruckus and called the police. I think that's what saved my life. I don't remember much of that."

"What was Jeremy after?"

"He'd stolen priceless artworks belonging to my father. Detective Brent thought my mother caught Jeremy. She struggled with him and died for the sake of art. When my father heard the commotion and came in, he was next on the Jeremy agenda.

"I was too late to help either of them when I arrived home unexpectedly before Jeremy was finished. Detective Brent put that much together when he realized he couldn't blame me." The sound of my bitterness echoed in my ears. Brent had put me through the paces when I was most vulnerable. *Thank goodness for Crystal.* "After the dust settled, I realized the place as well as the memories haunted me. Though my business was doing well there, I decided to move away and try for a fresh start. But it was hard starting over and leaving my aunt and the town where I'd lived my whole life. The suspicions and the legal struggle became the icing on the cake."

"How did you find this lawyer who saved you from arrest?"

"I called a judge who was a friend of my dad's. He recommended Crystal. When I called her, she came to the rescue and, believe me, she's worth every dollar I paid her. She's ruthless ... She showed me how to stand and be counted. Thanks to her, I survived the following months of interrogations, threats, 'the box' and a variety of nasty nightmares that plague me still."

His face remained shuttered. He merely nodded and asked nothing more before he left.

Chapter 11

THE PASSING DAYS and evenings had begun to show signs of spring. It wasn't long before snow and ice had melted into oblivion for another year. I found southern New Hampshire beautiful in April, though a minor snowstorm intruded now and again.

The roads were clear as I drove to the local high school on the edge of Schmitz Landing. I'd been invited to offer a tangle hour with the teachers, who were in dire need of a relaxation period. The end of the school year approached, exams and extra activities needed finishing, and the entire school staff felt the pressure.

One lonely parking spot at the end of the lot stood empty. I drove in, climbed out, locked the car, and hurried across the grounds. Mariette Harden met me at the door and showed me the way to the staff lounge where she introduced me to fifteen teachers. I wondered who controlled the kids while I taught these tired-looking people to relax.

Jenna Crown passed the tangling supply envelopes around. Everyone opened theirs and found tiles, a pen, pencil, and blending stump along with a small wrapped chocolate candy. I quickly explained the process, the benefits of tangling, and got everyone started on a tangle.

Quiet descended on us as teachers worked to develop their designs. I walked them through the steps with a demonstration of each section on their tile. I showed the shading technique using the pencil to add graphite to edges of line. When I blended with the paper stump to finish the project, it brought sounds of surprise from the group. I held each tile up for viewing before I formed a mosaic of them on the table. I clicked a photo with my cell phone and thanked everyone for participating.

A bell sounded. I could hear students bustle in the outside corridor. Teachers rose and readied to leave. One by one they offered remarks and laughter over their prized works of art. Soon, I was alone, packing my supplies and work board. The door behind me opened with a soft swish.

"You've done a great service. Thanks for coming," Mariette said as I hefted the supply bag to my shoulder.

I smiled, shook her hand, and walked with her along the corridor to the exit. We chatted amiably until we reached the double doors.

"Have the police found any further clues about Flora's killer?" Mariette asked with an innocent tone of voice.

I shrugged and said I hadn't heard a word. She stepped away and waved good-bye and left me thinking about why I hadn't heard from, or seen Jonah in a week or more. Could it be his interest in me had waned, or was he avoiding me?

I reasoned life becomes busy, people have priorities, and I wasn't one of Jonah's.

Two miles from the center of town, the sky opened up. Heavy rain pelted the windows and pounded the roof of my car. Thunder was followed by lightning strikes. Visibility was nil so I reduced my speed in the hope I'd arrive home safely. Around a sharp curve, known as *Deadman's Bend,* a sheet of hail replaced the rain. The road disappeared from view. My car swerved into the guardrail, bounced off, and careened across the road.

The sound of metal against metal filtered into my brain as the car flipped up on its nose before somersaulting down the rocky hill toward the gully below.

My seatbelt tightened as I gripped the steering wheel. Inflated airbags smashed me from the front and sides before we landed with a thud. The MINI Cooper rocked a bit … and stilled.

My heart pounded. I fought through deflated airbag debris to check my body parts for damage. I gasped for oxygen and released the seatbelt that choked the daylights out of me. The windshield, though cracked into a gazillion spiderweb lines, had held. I glanced through the side windows to take stock of my surroundings.

The storm had passed in a speedy torrent, leaving a path of wreckage in its wake. I stayed in the car ... A sudden pounding on the window brought my aching head around. Jonah yelled at the top of his lungs.

Why? I was in shock, not deaf.

"Are you okay? Can you get out? Unlock the doors," he insisted.

I nodded, granted his request, and opened the driver side door to peer out. Soggy, sponge-like moss lay puddled over my feet as I slid from the seat onto terra firma. Jonah made his way to me, all the while repeating his 'are you okay?' mantra. His eyes were filled with fear, his face with a mixture of concern and relief.

He helped me stand then wrapped me in a bear hug.

I stepped back, brushed my hands across my face and said, "I'm all right, really. I'm sorry. I lost control of the car when the hail struck."

"You're sure?" He peered into my face, looked over my shoulder at the car, and shook his head. "Your car didn't fare as well. Good thing Coopers have super safety features. He stared hard at me and then smirked. "You'll have a few bruises, though. The bag hit your face hard."

My hand in his, we started up the slippery incline. Without a backward glance at the sturdy little car, I hiked the mucky terrain. At road level, flashing lights appeared. His police cruiser, a rescue vehicle, and a fire truck stood lined up on the side of the road. Jonah spoke with the team as EMTs escorted me to the rescue truck and inspected me for injury.

I waited impatiently as reports were finished and then I signed the sheet refusing medical treatment. After that, I sat on the bumper of a car and watched Jonah.

His head together with Jim Haggerty's, Jonah pointed to the guardrail, then to the embankment. Jim, the rescue team's crew chief nodded, gazed at the swath of broken bushes, and glanced at me. Jonah left him shaking his head, and returned to me.

"Luckily, for you I was returning from giving testimony at the court house when I saw the damage to the guardrail and thought I ought to take a look. Tell me, why didn't you allow them to transport you to the hospital? You should be checked out. Your face is bruising. You were lucky to avoid major injuries, Katarina."

I was past caring that he called me by my given name and I was glad he'd found me. It felt like months since he'd kissed me, but Jonah was all business now, his attitude impersonal and professional.

"No need to see some doctor who'll tell me to take two aspirin and call if I'm not better tomorrow. Besides, I've got things to take care of, including transportation. Thankfully, I can walk nearly everywhere I need to go."

"I can see you plan to be stubborn about this, so I'll give you a lift home. A wrecker is on the way to remove the car from the gully. Tell your insurance people they can view it at Judd's Storage outside of town."

I thanked him as Jonah escorted me to the police car. Before I got in, I stepped to the edge of the slope and glimpsed my beaten MINI Cooper. Tears caught in my throat at the thought of my second escape from death. *How many lives did I have?*

"Get in the car, Katie. Now," Jonah ordered.

Numb, I nodded and slid onto the front seat of the cruiser. The ride home was a silent affair. His attention focused on the road, Jonah answered the police radio every now and then. Otherwise he was silent. When we arrived at the house, he entered the drive and stopped in front of the garage.

"Rest today. No antics, or business stuff. Understand?" he ordered when we entered my kitchen.

"I'm fine. I know I'll be sore tomorrow, but right now,

I'm okay."

"You say that, but you haven't seen the color breaking out on your face. Would you like me to inspect your body for other bruises?" Jonah grinned.

This was the first personal action I'd gotten from him in too long. Relief washed over me.

"I think I can handle things from here. Thanks for the offer, though," I answered with a giggle. "Any word on Flora's investigation?"

"I've hit bottom." He set the kettle to boil and ran his hand over his cropped hair. "Who'd have thought a person could make as many enemies as Flora had? It's mind-boggling. If I put every single person who disliked her, in 'the box,' I'd be there for three months." He snorted and took cups from the cupboard.

"I could help you by asking around ... If you don't mind? People are more apt to talk to me than to a police detective. The badge scares them."

"It doesn't seem to faze you," he exclaimed.

"I'm different. Most folks haven't gone where I've been. I hope they never have to go there, either."

"The person who killed Flora isn't about to take kindly to your snooping. I'd rather you didn't get involved, for safety's sake, if for no other reason."

"I am involved. I'm a suspect, even though you don't want me to be. Let me help."

"No, and that's final. Understand?" He nearly shouted the words. I stepped into his space.

"You're sure you don't want my assistance?" I ran a hand along his jacket collar.

His laughter cheered me. He took a step back. "You're something else. Just stay out of my investigation. I have enough to worry about without wondering if you'll be knocked off next."

I lifted a shoulder and hoped I passed off a look of innocence. "Sure, if that's what you want."

The kettle whistled. Jonah made tea and I gratefully took the proffered cup. The cozy chair beckoned. I snuggled into

82   *J.M. Griffin*

its soft cushions.

"Don't think for a minute that I believe you've agreed to leave things alone," he said. "You have a streak of independence that tells me you're about to embark on your own inquiry."

With a chuckle, I sipped the brew then leaned my elbows on my knees.

Curiosity got the better of me. "Who is your most likely suspect?"

"Other than you?" He thought for a second and said, "Flora was a woman of secrets. I've learned several of them and know there are more. If she kept a journal or diary that could point the way, I haven't found it. To answer your question, I believe one of your students has something to hide. Flora could have been taunting her with that."

"So it's a woman, then?"

He tipped his head slightly and answered. "Bill has a solid alibi for the night in question. Gretchen does, too. Francine, and the others have alibis that can't be corroborated. I don't consider Freda a suspect, but to be truthful, any one of them, even an elderly lady, could have committed murder — with help."

Surprised, I shook my head. Freda couldn't drag a woman who outweighed her by at least fifty to sixty pounds. The idea was ridiculous. A conversation we'd had in class ran through my head.

"One day, just before the students left, we discussed Flora. Though Janet was shaken over Flora's death she said she wasn't sorry the woman was gone. She said Flora was mean, that she caused pain and humiliation for others. Most of us agreed with her. When I pressed her for a reason why she felt that way Freda stopped her before she could answer, though she'd started to speak. After that, everyone left, and I forgot all about it."

"You're sure it was Janet and not Francine?"

"Why? Do you know something about Francine that would incriminate her? Francine is a librarian. She'd never hurt a fly."

"Honey, just because she's a librarian, doesn't mean she couldn't be Flora's killer. Librarians can also become stressed.

Maybe Flora pushed the wrong buttons and Francine snapped. She is a nervous sort."

"Flighty would be a better fit for her," I said with a smile. "I still think you're wrong about Francine. Janet doesn't seem a killer either."

"Let me ask you this, did Jeremy seem like a killer before your parents' murder?"

A cold chill skittered along my spine. I'd begun to lift my teacup and my arm froze in place. I stared at Jonah. He was right. Never in my life would I have thought Jeremy capable of such brutality.

"You have a point," I murmured.

"When we last spoke, you said you have nightmares. Tell me about them."

Had he produced his notepad, our conversation would have ended, but instead, Jonah was now showing me a different side to his nature, one I felt comfortable with. Finally, someone cared about my feelings.

"I have a recurring dream of Jeremy's assault. I could never get past the sight of his knife tearing at me. I couldn't identify the wielder of it. The doctor promised it would come forward one day and he was right. Since I've remembered those were Jeremy's actions, I'm sleeping better. I think it's the one thing I have Flora to thank for. If she hadn't been strangled and left on the bench, I'd probably still be having *the dream.*"

Jonah glanced at his watch when his cell phone rang. He answered, listened, and said he'd be right there. Without a word of explanation, he rose and donned his coat.

"Duty calls?" I asked with a smirk.

"Never a dull moment in this tiny metropolis." He sighed. "I thought I'd be bored after working in the Big Apple." He snorted and stepped close to me, running his hands over my arms.

"I know you wouldn't normally have told me what happened, but I'm glad you did. No wonder you left Ohio." He leaned into me with a deep, warm kiss. I melted inside, not wanting the moment to end.

Jonah stepped away and said, "I'm sorry I've been persistent and aggravating. I have a job to do. Lifting every rock and prying things apart to find clues are part of it."

He'd done that, and then some, where I was concerned. Could I really trust him, or had my heart opened me up for betrayal? He'd come to my rescue, hours before ... I not only wanted to kiss him, but the idea of tearing his clothes off and having passionate sex with him had presented itself more times than I cared to admit. These thoughts and others like them sent a tingle along my nerves and tickled my stomach — not to mention other parts.

"I have to go, I'll stop by later to check on you. You may feel okay now, but after being tossed around like you were, I guarantee you'll be sore later." Jonah brushed my forehead with his lips and left by way of the kitchen.

I watched him enter the cruiser and back it from the driveway. A driveway without my MINI Cooper ... I tried to put the accident out of my mind and instead, focus on what he'd said about the murder and his investigation.

Jonah's theories on Flora's journaling made sense. Wouldn't she keep a record of secrets she'd learned in order to remember details to taunt those who crossed her path?

I'd flung my coat on a nearby chair and now carefully shrugged into it. My muscles had begun to ache — crying out for a warm bath. Jasmine mewed, looked at her food dishes, and then at me.

Hurriedly, I filled the water bowl and tossed some cat crunchies in the other dish before I scooted out to see Gretchen. I knew if I didn't deal with this now I might be too sore later.

Chapter 12

I ROTATED MY left shoulder, to ease a persistent ache, then glanced at my watch as I entered the salon. The chairs were empty and nobody waited their turn for beautification. Wide mirrors covered one wall of hairstyling stations. I glanced over, noticed my facial bruises, winced at my reflection, and then called out a 'hello.'

A return call echoed from the rear of the salon. The resident nail technician stepped around the corner, took one look at my face, and nervously asked what she could do for me.

"Is Gretchen about?"

"She's gone for the day. Her last appointment left a little while ago. I think she's home." The girl thumbed toward the bakery a few doors down. "You could try her there."

I thanked her and sped down the sidewalk to the entry of the apartments above the bakery. I swung the door inward and found Gretchen descending the last two stairs.

"Wow, what happened to you?" Gretchen asked, her eyes wide.

I responded with a smirk. "I had an accident this afternoon, totaled my car, and the airbags gave me a facial."

"Cripes, you look awful. Were you hurt?"

"No, just scared. It started to rain and then turned to hail. I lost control of the car and that's that. Do you have a minute to talk?"

"All right. Join me at the café and we can chat there."

"I'd rather not go there if you don't mind."

Gretchen hesitated, then grabbed my arm and ushered me

up the staircase into her apartment. "Stay here, I'll be right back."

Before I could ask where she was going, I heard her thump down the stairs and the door slam shut behind her. I slid my jacket off, searched for a place to hang it, and ended up tossing it on the far end of the sofa.

The cheerful décor of her rooms appealed to me. The living room opened to a small galley kitchen outfitted with two stools and a counter bar. Gingham curtains hung in the windows and a pot of pink begonias balanced on the sill.

I heard Gretchen come in and call to me. I sauntered back to the living room and smiled at the sight of a loaf of French bread accompanied by a bag — probably filled with pastry. I suddenly realized how hungry I was.

"What do you have to go with the bread?" I wondered aloud.

"I made a pan of eggplant parmesan yesterday. Want some?"

"You bet." I grinned, rubbed my hands together, and settled in for a meal.

Between bites, Gretchen asked, "What brings you here?"

I swallowed a mouthful of the best eggplant parmesan I'd ever tasted and said, "Do you know where Flora lived?"

Her expression curious, she said, "Sure, her house is on Dillary Lane. Why?"

"Can we go by there after dark?"

"*Good gravy!* Don't tell me you want to break into her house?" A peel of laughter burst from her as her eyes grew bright. "You've finally decided to take the investigation of Flora's death into your own hands, haven't you? The cops haven't come up with any good leads?"

"Yes and no. I figure Flora must have kept a journal of sorts. Men don't know where we'd keep things of that nature, so I thought I'd take a look and wondered if you'd be interested in coming along as backup? Wouldn't it make sense for Flora to have kept some kind of notes on the secrets she had learned about people?"

Gretchen's head bobbed up and down while I talked. Her excitement was palpable and I grinned over her enthusiasm.

"Katie, she must have had volumes considering how many people disliked her. When word spread that you'd found her dead and that you topped the suspect list, someone suggested you get a medal if you proved to be the one that knocked her off. That's how the locals felt about her."

"So, you're in on this caper, then?" I asked.

"I can't let you go alone ... So yes, count me in. What time do you want to leave? Dillary Lane isn't far from here. We can walk."

I warmed to the idea. "Good because my car won't be going anywhere soon. Around seven should be good. There's a spring rally in the town square tonight. We won't be conspicuous on the street. Wear dark clothes and bring a flashlight with you. Do you know if Flora had an alarm system in her house?"

Gretchen shook her head. "I don't think so. She had a miserable dog that's been given to the pound now that she's dead. She bragged about how good a watchdog he was. She kept a key hidden under a frog in the flower garden, too. Flora wasn't aware I knew that."

"Great, that'll simplify things. I'd hate to have to break a window to get inside."

Her laughter and mine collided.

Gretchen became serious. "Where did you come up with this idea, anyway? It's an interesting concept."

"If you must know, Detective Kilbride mentioned he thought Flora had kept a journal or diary of sorts. That's when I considered breaking into her house. Women know women's habits better than any man ever could. I thought you'd like to tag along."

"Then tell me why you didn't want to go to the café? Afraid someone would hear our plans?"

I hesitated for a fraction of a second before I answered her. Jonah's suspicions of Janet and Francine were definitely not for anyone else's ears.

"That's exactly why. And my face is bruised and I look a wreck ... But really, I wouldn't want someone to call the police and tell them what we're planning. Jonah's just beginning to trust me." I wish I'd left that out, but the words jumped off my tongue before I could stop them. I dragged my coat on, shivered, and wished warmer weather would arrive soon. I promised I'd return for Gretchen by seven.

Before I could close the door, Gretchen grinned and said, "I guess you and the handsome detective are growing closer?"

I chuckled and admitted, "Sometimes, I think so. Other times, not so much." With a shrug, I sped down the stairs.

Luscious aromas accosted my sense of smell upon my entry to the bakery. Bread, cakes, pies, and assorted pastry lay in display cases, begging to be eaten. I ordered a loaf of Asiago bread and a couple Danish pastries 'to go.' I hurried home with my bundles tucked in my arms.

Time slipped away and before I knew it, the clock ticked nearly seven o'clock. I'd managed to wash the few dishes in the sink, speak with my insurance agent about my accident, and get dressed for breaking and entering. When I'd been known as the budding artist extraordinaire, I'd worn black all the time.

Once my parents had passed on to the great yonder, I'd never worn black again. The color depressed me, even though I designed my tangles with a black pen on a white surface. Dressing in the dark colors felt different than using them in art.

Dark gloves warmed my hands, and a navy blue pea coat covered my black slacks and jersey. A crowd had gathered on the green, bundled in winter attire. Temperatures still dropped low at night in April. As I scurried along the pavement to Gretchen's a car slowed and stopped across the street. I cast a sideway glance to see Jonah staring at me from his car.

"Going somewhere?" he asked with one eyebrow hitched higher than the other.

"Gretchen and I are about to go to the square for the spring celebration," I called across the road.

"Thought you'd be cozy with your cat, in front of the fire by now … Don't do anything strenuous while you're there. Promise me."

"I wouldn't think of it. I'm already feeling the effects of today's tumble down the embankment," I fibbed. Tomorrow would be when I'd be really sore.

"Have an early night then, will you?"

"Sure thing, Detective," I promised, with my fingers and toes crossed.

He drove off and turned left at the intersection.

Gretchen waited for me just inside the stairwell. Electricity all but jumped off her when I opened the door.

"Was that Kilbride you were talking to? I didn't want to come out if it was. I was afraid he'd figure out what we're up to."

I laughed. "Nervous, are you? He thinks we're going to the spring celebration. If you're ready, let's go. Did you bring a flashlight?"

She nodded, pulled a small flashlight from her pocket, and pointed to the corner of the street.

"We'll cut through Park Street and then take Merry Lane to Dillary. Ready?"

I sauntered along beside her as song broke out in the crowded park across from us.

We made it to Dillary without incident. Gretchen lifted the garden frog and dug at the key frozen to the ground. When she couldn't lift it from its place, she motioned me over to help. I held the frog while she used the edge of her flashlight to pry the key from its place.

Old neighborhood homes sat far apart. This area had been the first settled in Schmitz Landing. Quaint street lamps filtered soft light along the sidewalks but didn't glow bright enough to reach up yards or driveways. Cloaked in near darkness, we approached the house.

Gretchen slid the key in the door and clicked the lock open. She went in first and I followed. Drawn curtains held the house in total darkness. Gretchen said Flora was obsessive about her privacy and always kept the curtain closed. Maybe she feared peeping Toms or she didn't want anyone to know *her* business the way she knew theirs.

I flashed the concentrated beam of light around the room while Gretchen entered the next one. We searched places where we'd have considered hiding a journal. Coming up empty, we climbed to the second floor of the petite chalet-style house. I veered to the room on the left and Gretchen took the bedroom to the right.

I was sliding the mirror above the dresser aside when I heard an exclamation from across the hall.

"Come here! You're not gonna believe what I found," Gretchen said in a loud whisper.

I tripped over the threshold and sprawled on the floor before I could catch my balance. Gretchen's laughter brought on a fit of my own. My anxiety released and we both giggled.

"Graceful, aren't you?" She snickered. "Some B&E artist you'd make. Honestly."

"Never mind that, what did you find that's so important?" I demanded.

She walked to the small fireplace in the wall. Ornate, carved plinth blocks framed the opening — birds with outstretched wings perched on either side of the mantel as though they'd recently landed there. Gretchen pulled the body of one bird. A door to a compartment in the carved blocks snapped open as a solid unit. With her flashlight focused on the interior, Gretchen reached in and pulled out three leather volumes, one a bit thicker than the others. I leaned forward to peer over her shoulder.

I said, "Those look interesting. Let's take a look at them."

"Yeah, but not here. We should leave before we get caught," Gretchen whispered. "Let's go." She closed the panel and tucked the books inside her jacket.

We made our way downstairs. We'd almost reached the door when it opened. Jonah stood facing us, a look of astonishment on his face.

"This doesn't look like the Village Green to me, ladies." He swore, stepped inside, and slammed the door behind him. In an instant, he flicked the light switch to illuminate the entry.

"What the hell are you doing here and how did you get in?"

Gretchen backed into me as I moved back against the wall. I stowed my flashlight in my pocket and stepped around her to answer Jonah's question with one of my own.

"Why are you here, Detective?"

"Investigating, that's why. I advised you not to involve yourself, didn't I?"

I blustered. "W-well, yes, sort of. I was curious about Flora's house and Gretchen showed it to me. We were just leaving."

His lips tightened. His face grew hard and cold as he stared at the two of us. He issued a sigh and asked, "Did you find what you were looking for?"

"No, we didn't," Gretchen said as I opened my mouth and closed it just as quickly.

"There are no secret hiding places filled with notebooks or a diary?" he asked.

"Not that we could find. Sorry. We didn't get to search the basement, though," Gretchen added.

"Don't bother. There's nothing down there except cobwebs." His gaze slowly wandered over us as he seemed to make a decision.

"Come on, I'll take you both home. Don't come here again. How did you get in?"

Gretchen held up the key, which he swiped from her hand. She curled her fingers and stuffed her hand into her pocket with a huff of air.

"Come along." He escorted us to the car and waited until we were both seatbelted in before he drove from the curb. I pinched Gretchen and she pinched me back and gave me a half grin.

We arrived at Tangled Wings in a matter of minutes. Jonah waited until we all entered my studio. His face was now granite-like in nature. I grew wary that he suspected we had found the proof he needed in Flora's house. Rather than question us, he ranted on awhile about our crime and that should he ever catch us again, he'd arrest us and toss our butts in jail.

Not one to be intimidated by cops, especially after I'd been bullied so many times in the past, I stepped up and said, "Don't threaten us, Detective. We get your point."

"Kat, I'm warning you. Don't do another stupid thing like this again. There's still a murderer out there. Don't you understand that?"

Gretchen stood next to me. "We do, and we promise it won't happen again. We're sorry." She nudged me with her elbow. Begrudgingly, I nodded in agreement.

Unsure if we'd convinced him of our sincerity, I waited for another outburst of temper. When it didn't happen, I breathed in relief and waited for him to leave.

"Do you realize how dangerous your actions were tonight?" he asked in a calmer tone.

Our heads bobbed in unison as we agreed that we'd been foolish. *Foolish enough to get caught, anyway.* With fingers looped in his belt, Jonah stared at us for a time. It was almost as though I could see the wheels turning in his head. He evaluated us, shook his head in despair, and left in a snit with a promise of arrest should there be a next time.

When his car sped down the street, I leaned against the work table, aware how weak-kneed I'd become. Bravery is one thing . . .

To be caught in the act of breaking the law, is another. If only we'd left a few minutes earlier, Jonah would have missed us completely. I slipped off my jacket and gloves as Gretchen did the same. Then, with books firmly in hand, she laid them out on the table.

We gazed at the leather bindings and panels of rich burgundy engraved with gold. One book, thicker than the other two, held our attention.

"Should we read them now, or should we turn them over to Jonah?" I asked while I ran my fingertips across the grainy leather.

Gretchen's eyes were round and wide when she looked at me. "Are you nuts? We should read them. If we hand them over to Jonah, he'll arrest us. I don't plan on sitting in a jail cell, do you?"

"No, you're right. After all, isn't that why we stole them in the first place?" Common sense prevailed. At least, I thought it did. "Well, go ahead then. You take one and I'll check another."

I waited for her to make the first move. Gretchen slid her hand along the binding of the thinnest book before she snatched her hand away.

"Maybe we shouldn't read them. Maybe I don't want to know all the nasty secrets Flora had on the townsfolk. Look where it got her? Deader than dead."

"Right, but we could find out who had the worst secret to hide and that would lead to Flora's killer. Right?" I pointed out.

"Sure, it might, but what if the real killer isn't the person with the worst secret, but one who'd been pushed too hard and snapped? Have you considered that?"

"Now that you mention it, that also makes sense." I slanted a look at Gretchen and asked, "What do you suggest we do with them, then?"

"We should destroy them, that's what."

Aghast, I gaped at Gretchen with my head wagging right and left like a dog's tail.

"We can't do that. It might be important evidence." I stacked the books and pushed them away from us.

Then what's your idea, Miss Smartypants?" Gretchen asked in a snide tone.

I shrugged a shoulder. "We could package them up and send them to Jonah's attention at the police station."

A shake of her head met the suggestion. I waited for Gretchen to reconsider the notion.

"Let's have a glass of wine and talk this over," she said.

I took the books, shut off the studio lights, and headed to the kitchen with Gretchen close behind. Once our wine glasses were filled with rich burgundy, we sat and stared at the journals. While the idea of searching Flora's house for them had seemed a good one when I'd proposed it to Gretchen, we had come to a crossroad and couldn't determine which direction to take.

After we drank two bottles of wine, we came to the conclusion that we'd painted ourselves into a tight corner. We couldn't give the books to Jonah, nor could we return them to Flora's.

"Jonah's gonna be angry if we *shend* them to him," Gretchen slurred. "He'll know we took 'em. Then he'll yell at *ush* again, or we could get *arreshted*. I don't have bail money."

Too much wine can loosen tongues that are frequently out of control at the best of times. This instance was one of them.

"I have bail money, plenty of bail money. Don't worry," I muttered.

"Where'd you get bail money?" Gretchen chuckled and swept her hair back from her forehead.

"I'm rich." After I hiccupped the words, I knew I'd made a huge blunder. Too much wine, or anything else is bad, very bad.

Her eyes popped wide open and she cackled.

Yep, we were toasted from our adventure and drinking — I sobered a tad after my verbal mistake.

"You aren't rich. You're a working *shlob* like the *resht* of *ush*." Her speech had taken a turn for the worse and I wondered if I sounded the same.

"Let's sleep on it tonight and make a decision in the morning. What do you say?"

"Okay, good idea. I'm gonna relax on the *shofa*. Breaking and entering is tiring." Gretchen laughed, flopped on the sofa, and nodded off.

Once she was covered with a couple afghans, I set the fireplace on low to keep her warm, and gathered the books under my arm. Step by step, I climbed to the second floor, the bundle under my arm, and a hand on the rail to guide me upward. Jasmine sat at the top of the stairs, her gaze unwavering. When I reached her, she offered an indifferent sniff and marched down the hall ahead of me.

Aside from the fact that I'd had too much to drink — I didn't usually imbibe too much alcohol — I was curious about the books' contents.

A lounged on the bed, pillows piled behind my back, and

played my fingers across the covers again.

No bad vibes tightened my nerves, but I wasn't psychic, so why would I expect to feel vibes of any kind? I snickered and pulled the thinnest book forward. Carefully, I lifted the cover. A huge breath whistled past my lips at what lay on those inside pages.

To say I was horrified by her joy and hatefulness over being privy to others mistakes, would be an understatement. Halfway through her verbal abuse of people I didn't know, I slapped the journal shut. The other two volumes lay beside me on the bed.

After scanning a few pages of each, I leaned back, lost in thought while I gazed at the starry sky through my bedroom windows. How had I been stupid enough to think I could solve this mystery? Who, of Flora's many victims, had thought to implicate me in the murder of such a pathetic woman? Why would a person want to hurt others? By hurting them, did she make herself feel better, superior in some way?

Chapter 13

SOME THINGS SHOULD be left alone. Some should be dealt with by those capable, and some shouldn't be brought to light at all. The wicked snatches of disparaging gossip and innuendo I found in Flora's books were often accompanied by scribbled illustrations. Her glee over the misery of others disturbed and fascinated me at the same time.

Flora was a sad woman with a tawdry life. Her unhappiness unfolded within the journal pages. By the time I'd gotten to the middle of the first book and peered at the pictures, shame overtook me. A voyeur, that's what I'd become, just as Flora had been.

I'd read her stories, or lies, concerning neighbors and once close friends. What a sorry person she'd grown into. Her fervor for taunting others was ever present in her writing.

I could almost hear her speak the words as she wrote them. One by one she'd turned friend into foe with no mercy for any of them. How she'd survived this many years came as a surprise.

I must have nodded off because I awoke to the phone ringing, the blare of the alarm, and somebody pounding on the downstairs door.

I staggered from bed, half-asleep and still dressed from the previous night. By the time I reached the kitchen, Jasmine stood on the countertop, her paws splayed across the sink window. Gretchen stirred from sleep.

Bleary-eyed, she sat up, thrust off the covers, and muttered, "What the hell. Can't anybody sleep around here?"

My laughter bubbled over at her disheveled appearance and

rude comment. I swung the door wide and Jonah marched inside.

"What's this, a sleepover?" he asked, followed by a smirk.

"Too much wine and late hours. Coffee?" I offered.

While I brewed coffee, Gretchen stumbled to the studio bathroom. Jonah lifted the crocheted afghans off the floor. He tossed them on the sofa and turned to me, when his eyes widened.

"You should see your face. It's a myriad of color."

I scurried to the nearest mirror and checked out the hues. Rainbows had nothing on my cheek bones or the bridge of my nose. My eyes weren't swollen, but were smudged with shadows.

"Great. Now I'll be the talk of the town." I sighed as Jonah snickered.

"It looks like you got crazy with a makeup brush and too much color." He stared at the wine bottles on the table, the empty glasses nearby, and his grin widened.

"Did you two celebrate not being arrested last night after I left?"

I poured steaming brew into cups, set out milk and sugar, pointed to it and him. "You could say we had a little too much to drink, though I don't have a hangover." No, but I hoped Gretchen didn't remember my remarks about having more money than I needed.

Gretchen, refreshed and looking better, strode in, picked her coffee cup off the table, and flounced onto a chair.

"Do you always make early house calls, Detective?" she asked.

"When I have to, yes." He flicked a glance at each of us, motioned for me to take a chair, and then sat at the end of the rectangular table.

"You didn't go out again last night, then?"

I quickly assessed his attitude. He wasn't all business, but his countenance wasn't friendly either. I offered Gretchen a slight nod and answered Jonah.

"We watched you leave, came in here, and drank ourselves into a stupor. Why do you ask? Has something happened?"

"You're sure neither of you left the house, then?"

Annoyed at his insistent question, I retorted, "Am I speaking a foreign language or are you not listening? We were here. Now, what's happened?"

"There's been a strangulation attempt using the same method as was used on Flora. So you see why I was curious."

I leapt from the chair, tipping it over. It crashed to the floor. Jasmine flew up the stairs, and I squealed, "Oh gosh. An attempt . . .not a murder, right?"

"How could we be? You just woke us up," Gretchen responded. "Where were you last night, then, Detective? Were you not prowling the streets like policemen should?"

He smirked, gave a slight snort at Gretchen's snarky return, and focused on me.

"Since a leather belt was used — the same as was used on Flora — I'd say somebody would like to lay the blame at your doorstep."

Tense, I asked, "Do you plan on telling us who this near *victim* is?"

"Her family was notified. I'm sorry to tell you this. Your student, Janet Latchkey, was nearly strangled to death."

Shocked, I covered my mouth with my hand while tears rolled down my cheeks. Gretchen rose, made a dash to the bathroom, and didn't immediately return.

"You're sure Janet's all right?" I mumbled as I caught my breath.

His hand closed over mine. Jonah nodded and said, "Very sure. I don't know what the hell is happening in this town, but I'll find out."

My caffeinated brain rode a track as fast as a car at the Indy 500. In light of what I'd read in the first journal, I wondered if Janet might have seen something or overheard a conversation that resulted in her becoming next in line for the killer. What could she have seen, or heard, and from whom — or about whom? The question plagued me like a poison ivy rash that needs scratching.

"I have something to tell you, just not now," I whispered.

Gretchen walked down the hall, her face bleak and pale. With hands shaking, she glanced at the clock and announced she had to leave.

I walked her to the front door where she turned, hugged me, and murmured softly in my ear, "Try not to be upset. Jonah will sort this out."

With a nod, I waited until she reached the sidewalk before returning to Jonah.

"What's on your mind that you couldn't tell me in front of Gretchen?" he asked.

I took a swig of coffee and confessed. "When we went to Flora's last night, we searched the house for journals and whatnot. She was a secretive woman who held fear and threats over the heads of people who considered her their friend. It's a wonder she lived so long."

A sardonic gleam entered Jonah's eyes. "I take it you found something or you wouldn't be telling me this."

"It was more the way she lived and how her house was set up that made me aware of her discontent. When drapes are closed day and night from fear of others finding out about life within the walls, there's a problem. Gretchen told me Flora constantly kept her drapes drawn, and had a guard dog to deter visitors."

"And?"

Unwilling to own up about the journal theft, I lifted open hands and shrugged. "She was strange that way. She had secrets of her own, not only everybody else's."

"So whose business did she know and how did she acquire the knowledge?"

I'm weak when it comes to keeping my lips buttoned. I know it. I work hard at learning to stay mum, but there it is. I just don't always know when to shut up.

"Her avid interest in the affairs of others began early in life. Not after she was thrown over by the original owner of this house, but long before that."

Jonah's blue eyes gleamed while the scar at the corner of

his eye pinched. He smiled. "You know this *how*? And, no lies, please."

I bit my tongue as the realization struck me. I'd done it again, opened my mouth so words could spill out. Crap and double crap!

"I'm merely making an assumption based on gossip I've heard in the classroom."

"Liar, now try again." He spoke in a tone laced with a hint of steel.

"Honestly, you can't think I would know more than what I hear from my students? I rarely interact with the townsfolk, and now that Janet is temporarily out of circulation, I won't get the gossip from the café, either."

Jonah rolled his eyes, and then studied my face with an intensity that set my nerves jangling. "I don't believe you for a moment. Come clean now, or I'll add you to my list of suspects for this case too."

I imitated someone who might be scared. "Oooh, as frightening as that sounds, I'm not worried in the least about being your suspect or anyone else's."

Jonah leaned forward, resting his elbows on the table. "You could be the next person on the killer's agenda."

"Possibly, but not likely, if I'm to be arrested for the murders. You'll have to do better than that, Jonah."

His features hardened, intensified by frostier eyes. He spoke softly. "Don't push me, Katarina. I care about you, but I'm a cop from New York City, not a country bumpkin from the hayfields. I know how to interrogate, to reduce a person enough so they'll even admit to things they couldn't possibly have done."

My hackles rose, an automatic response to cop bullying tactics. If I'd been close to sharing the journals with him, the idea had flown out the window, never to be considered again.

I leaned against the chair back, folded my arms, and murmured, "Well, well, there you are. The real you, at last. I've been wondering when you'd show up. You see, I don't, for a moment, believe you care about me. It's always about the job, the holier-than-thou job of making people feel frightened, small, inept, like criminals — when they aren't, never were, and never will be. Glad to see the real you has arrived. Remember, this isn't New York, and I don't fear you. We're done, now get out."

I rose, opened the door, and waited for him to leave. I'd overstepped the bounds of cop and suspect with my attitude. His eyes sparked with anger. I'd struck a nerve and that satisfied me to no end.

He zipped his jacket, strolled to the door, slammed it shut, and yanked me to him.

"You couldn't be more mistaken." His mouth came down on mine, searing me with his kiss until I couldn't breathe.

My heart thumped an erratic beat, and blood sang in my veins. I could feel my knees tremble. I closed the narrow space between us while running would have been a better idea. Only fools walk into traps. I wasn't a fool.

A slip of paper couldn't have fit between our bodies. I returned his kisses, each becoming more ardent than the last. I couldn't help myself. Maybe I *was* a fool.

He pushed me away after what seemed a century of tongue kisses, teeth grinding, and lip smacking. With eyes passion filled, he stared into mine. I could feel sexual heat emanate from him and knew he was as aroused as I.

"You're the most beguiling, infuriating, irritating, sexy woman I've ever met. I could make love to you right now, but my *job* doesn't allow me to have sex with a suspect. Don't push me, Katarina, ever. When you smarten up and want to tell me the truth, call me."

He stormed out the door without a backward glance, leaving me hot and bothered, as bewildered by the passion between us, as I was by his last words.

I dashed upstairs, gathered the journals, tossed them to the back of a closet shelf and readied for class. My brain ran wild with thoughts of tearing Jonah's clothes off.

The scars that remained from the assault had diminished to faint lines after several cosmetic surgeries. Now I was less self-conscious about them when I was naked but I wondered how Jonah would perceive them. Not all men can handle disfigurement of any kind, scars or otherwise. Though, in the throes of passion, one might not care about scars, but more about the act of quenching an extreme thirst for pleasure and satisfaction.

Several students straggled in, followed by a few more only minutes later. The gray day appeared to affect everyone as much as it did me. With a wide smile, a bright attitude, and a new tangle design, I handed a stack of tiles to Bill and asked that he pass them along.

We worked for an hour or so before tea and conversation. Jill Crantz, a horse-faced woman with a French braid that hung to her waist, offered to set the kettle to boil while Gretchen wandered the room viewing the drawings.

With our mugs of tea, we gathered in the gallery to discuss another art showing. With a smirk, Jill asked, "Was that Jonah Kilbride I saw leave here earlier this morning?"

"Yes, he stopped by to talk about Janet. You know her, don't you? She's one of my students who waitresses at the café across the green." I motioned to the shop that was visible through the gallery's front window.

"What about Janet?" Bill wanted to know.

"I'm sorry, but I thought all of you knew that last night, Janet was assaulted the same way Flora was." I choked out the last few words and waited for reactions from the group.

Freda's tea mug hit the floor with a crash. Shards of porcelain bounced in all directions while liquid splattered everywhere.

Bill gasped in surprise as shock set in over the announcement. I watched Gretchen take in the scene. She studied the faces of each student as the news sank in.

With her hands aflutter, Francine's tall form swayed like a bough in a windstorm. Her face grew paler by the second. As she headed toward the floor, Gretchen, Bill, and I rushed to catch her, jostling one another in an effort to save her from a hard fall.

Bill reached for Francine's waist, caught her to him, and murmured something so soft only she could hear. He lowered her into the nearest chair while Brenna hurried into the restroom to return seconds later with a glass of water.

Gretchen tipped her head toward the door and left the room. I followed, not far behind, with the promise of returning with something stronger for Francine to drink.

Whiskey comes in handy now and then. A splash of amber brown liquid hit the bottom of the glass as the bottle shook in my hand. Gretchen stood inside the kitchen doorway, her face cold and sober.

"I suspect the news has made quite an impact on the crew, wouldn't you say?" she asked.

"When everyone came in so solemn this morning, I thought for sure they knew and were reluctant to speak of Janet's attack. *Crap and double crap!* Leave it to me to blab it." I sighed and leaned against the door casing, my eyes on Gretchen's face.

"You sure do have a way with words, I'll give you that." Gretchen snorted. "Blunt and to the point. Couldn't you have been more subtle when you told them? I thought Freda was about to have a heart attack, and Francine ... Well, enough said. And by the way, please leave out any gory details."

She turned from the doorway and strode ahead of me to the gallery. Shamed by my lack of subtlety, I entered the room and handed Francine the glass of whiskey.

"Here, this will bring color back to your face."

She swallowed it in one gulp, coughed, wheezed, and hauled in a deep breath. "Goodness, that's horrible tasting."

"Feel better?" I asked with a smirk.

Francine nodded. "Yes, thanks."

A chuckle rounded the room. I surveyed the group and waited for their questions to begin. A cacophony of voices filled the gallery, bouncing off the walls while they pounded me with questions.

"One at a time, please. I'll share what I know, just slow down," I pleaded.

Bill asked, "How did the event come about?"

"I don't know. Detective Kilbride came to ask if I'd heard or seen any commotion last night. He told me Janet was accosted in the alley behind the cafe. She's a lovely person, and I wish this hadn't happened to her."

Bill stated, "We need to know more, like why she was attacked and who might be next. Was it linked to Flora's death? Those are the questions I want answers to. I'm going to see Kilbride today."

"That's a great idea. Why don't we go together, Bill?" Freda piped up. Murmurs of assent followed.

Their consensus left me to wonder what Kilbride's reaction would be when faced by such an assortment of people. Would they seem like a lynch mob or maybe like the worried citizens they were? To see what happened when they approached Jonah — without him knowing — would be worth more gold than I could offer. I smiled at the thought.

A nod of approval from Gretchen lifted my spirits after I avoided inquiries over Jonah's suspects. Truthfully, I didn't know who was on the list other than Gretchen and me. Even then, I didn't consider us his *Number Ones*.

Chapter 14

L EFT WITH GRETCHEN after class ended, I waited for her thoughts. She never disappoints me, and this time was no different.

"Katie, does Kilbride have the journals?"

I shook my head and explained. "If I'd given them to him, he'd have been angrier than when he left this morning. Honestly, he ticked me off. I had every intention of handing them over, but he made me so angry that I changed my mind."

"What caused your upset?" she asked with a tiny grin.

Reading her smile to be one concerning a possible romance between me and the big lug, I exclaimed, "It was nothing like that. He tried heavy-handed questioning tactics, you know, threats and the like. I got mad and kicked him out. When he left, he said I should call him when I wanted to tell him the truth. Let's put the journals back in their hiding place. Then he can find them on his own."

Gretchen, with hand on her hip, slanted a look at me, followed by a snort in my direction. "If he couldn't find them before, what makes you think he'll find them at all?"

"You might intimate to him that Flora had weird hiding places in her house, built-in hidey holes maybe. What do you say?"

"You're really reaching now. Just put on your big-girl panties and own up, Katie. What can he do to you other than thank you for making his job easier?" She laughed, raised an eyebrow and asked, "Did you read the journals?"

"Halfway through the first journal I was so appalled

I slapped it shut and tossed them all aside. Unable to leave them alone, I started the second one. She was a nasty woman, really nasty."

Warmed by the thought of gossip, her eyes sparkled with interest. She propped her chin in her hands, then idly rested her elbows on the work table and began to question me.

"What did she say? Anything about anyone we know?"

Shaking my head while Gretchen rubbed her hands together in anticipation, I stood firm. I said the book had been started in the years before either of us had moved to town and that Flora's writings had nothing to do with our crowd.

"What're you going to do with them then? I'm not about to have Kilbride put me under a microscope. I wouldn't hold up to an interrogation," Gretchen said.

"I'm going to put the books back — with or without you. That's my *big-girl panties'* decision. Help me or not, it's up to you."

With a grimace, Gretchen promised to consider taking part in another breaking and entering attempt. She commented that since we had surrendered Flora's house key, we'd have to become more creative. That was when I knew she'd join my adventure.

Late for work, Gretchen raced up the street. I watched her scoot along the walkway before I put the studio to rights. The return of the journals lay heavy on my mind, and I couldn't wait to get them out from under my roof.

Later in the day, I called the hospital, inquiring about Janet's condition. I was told she had been released. Curious over her attack, I rang her house. When the answering machine clicked on, I started to leave a message when Janet picked up the call.

Her voice was raspy as Janet said, "I'm here, Katie. I've been screening the calls. Jenkins has been bugging the daylights out of me for an interview. Honestly, I'm not up to being questioned by him."

"Detective Kilbride came by this morning to tell me of your attack. If you don't mind my asking, how did it happen?"

"Why don't you come by and we'll talk? There's something

I need to tell you."

Intrigued as I was by her invitation, I said, "I wouldn't want to disturb you. You should rest."

"I'll go nuts if I don't stay busy. I'm not used to doing nothing. Besides, I'll enjoy your company, so come over. I'll make tea. It'll be good for my throat."

Knowing she only lived a couple streets away from the studio, I agreed and headed over after replacing the phone in the charger.

I took the three steps up to Janet's front door and pressed the doorbell. The door opened instantly. Janet stood waving me inside, her eyes searching the neighborhood behind me.

Inside her home, I discarded my jacket while she threw the deadbolt with a click. I followed her into the living room, where she'd set up a tea service I'd seen before on a Martha Stewart commercial. A plate of tea biscuits, a sugar bowl with tongs, and a creamer nestled alongside the steaming pot. Two teacups with saucers completed the ensemble.

Janet directed me to take a seat across the coffee table from her. "You can't be too careful around here these days. That bitch Flora brought this on all of us, and I'm really angry at her. Never in my life would I hurt people the way Flora has. She deserved what she got, but why would I be next in line?"

"Tell me what happened," I said as she handed me a filled teacup. I sipped the heavenly Lady Grey brew.

"After the café closes the staff does the light clean-up. I don't usually work that late, but one of the women had a sick child and needed time off, so I picked up the extra hours. The owner has a company come in to clean windows and floors, but staff does the rest.

"It had been slow after nine, which allowed us to get things squared away. I took the bags of trash from the kitchen out to the dumpster at the end of the alley. On my second trip, I'd just thrown the bags into the bin when someone caught me around the neck and started to choke me." She sipped her tea and drew a deep breath.

My cup began to rattle in the saucer. Hastily, I set it on the table and propped my elbows on my knees to keep from shaking off the chair. Her account chilled me to the bone.

"Go on." I studied her. Janet wore a turtleneck jersey that wasn't folded but slumped loosely under her chin.

She offered the tea biscuits, but I shook my head and waited.

Her voice had become hoarser than when we'd spoken on the phone. Janet continued, "About a year ago, Penny had this woman come into our yoga class to teach us how to evade an attacker. I'm not sure what the course was called, but I'm glad I took it. I learned how to protect myself. You know, Katie, you have to be quick-witted to survive that kind of attack."

I smirked at her words. She was so right about that.

"Nobody can call you slow-witted now, can they?" I asked with a smile.

"No, they can't. At first I tried to get my hands under the belt. When I couldn't manage that, I used my last several seconds of consciousness to run my foot down the attacker's shinbone. I heard a yelp, the belt loosened, and I pushed my body backward with all my strength. We landed on the ground, but the bastard recovered and got away before I could get my act together."

I reached out and took her hand as she went to fill my teacup once more. "I'm so sorry this happened to you, I really am."

She reached up, pulled the turtleneck away from her neck, and showed me the dark bruised skin. The belt had cut into the soft tissue, leaving a raw mark. I could feel my chest tighten in anguish over her terrible experience.

"When I get my hands on that creep, I'll repay the pain he caused me with the belt. Honest to God, I thought my life was over. The end, you know?"

"Yes, I know," I mumbled. "What happened after you caught your breath?"

"While on the ground I gasped for air like a fish does. I heard footsteps receding. I just couldn't get up right away. I guess fear or lack of oxygen does that. Anyway, one of the staff came out to see where I'd gotten to and found me trying to get off the ground, the belt still around my neck. I scared the bejeepers out of her, too. She called the cops after she helped me inside. Your friend, Jonah Kilbride, came and took the report."

"So, what did you want to tell me besides all that? Is there something special you remembered?"

"The smell, I remembered the smell of the person. It was strange. My attacker wore the same scent that Flora wore all the time. Kind of fruity, it was. I can't identify it exactly, so don't ask me to try. Should I tell Detective Kilbride?"

I nodded. "Absolutely, he'll want to know that and anything else you remember." I sipped the cooled tea, nibbled a biscuit, and felt relief flow over me like a warm blanket. Janet was alive and angry as hell. Which was good. It meant she was on the mend, wouldn't allow the assault to stop her from living her life ... and I knew if she ever figured out the identity of the killer, that person would be in a world of hurt when she finished with them.

"I'm proud of you, Janet, for fighting back and surviving the assault. Rest until you're ready to return to work and don't let this keep you down. When I told the students about your attack today, they were very concerned and they headed out to grill Jonah about the incident. I'd loved to have been a fly on that wall."

She smiled for the first time since I'd arrived. "He's a nice man and your students are good people. I listened to their well wishes on the answering machine and figured someone had spoken to them. I'll give the police station a call later and let Detective Kilbride know about the smell."

After a few more words of sympathy and wishing her well, I slipped my jacket on and bid her farewell. Janet's story left me feeling a tad jumpy, and wondering who would be next.

I stopped at the bakery for rolls and sauntered down

the street, thinking hard about the fragrance Janet remembered. What could it be? Was it sweet, pungent, or honeyed?
Bewildered by her admission, I couldn't put my finger on what
niggled me about that.

Entering the house, I found Jasmine waiting for a snack.
I fed her and then heated soup and made a sandwich for my
own repast.

In the following days, spring burst upon Schmitz Landing by
way of tulips, daffodils, and jonquils. Classes moved forward
and Janet returned. I taught regularly at the Wellness Center.
A few new students registered at the studio and settled in with
the regulars.

My yoga class sessions ran out but I re-registered and felt
better for it. Flora's journals lay unread, but beckoned me from
the closet as life became busier than ever. Gretchen and I hadn't
been able to coordinate a return time so I could rid myself of
their heavy burden. I fought the morbid temptation to read
more of them — I knew no good would come of that. I didn't
want to know anyone else's secrets, especially when I didn't
want mine known.

Jonah cruised by the studio without stopping. He didn't
arrive unannounced or make an effort to contact me. I missed
our sparring, his kisses, the feel of his body pressed up against
me. I shook my head and worked off thoughts that could only
lead to disenchantment. Cops love one thing, the law. They're
married to their job, choosing it over everything and everyone else.

A new design on canvas, and central to the upcoming
gallery display, was secured to my easel. Fine linen, covered
with numerous coats of gesso and sealer made for easy pen
work. Black ink on a white background with a touch of sepia
for interest, I viewed the drawing with pleasure. Working from
the center outward, I'd finished one section of the piece and

now concentrated on the next.

The incessant ringing of the phone caused an *oops* moment, where my pen slanted in a direction I hadn't planned. O*ops* were incorporated into opportunities in drawings. I often told students that there were no mistakes, only opportunities in this art. That eased their minds when they thought they'd drawn something the wrong way. 'There is no wrong way either,' I'd say with a smile.

If only life's *oops* were as easy to rectify.

"Hello?" I answered the phone before it drove me nuts.

"This is Detective Brent. Is that you, Ms. Granger?"

I recognized his voice from my past. My heart rapped against my ribs and I felt flushed as anxiety, rather than blood, roared through my system.

With a deep breath, I asked, "What can I do for you, Detective?"

"Just wanted to let you know a Detective Kilbride requested and has been sent a copy of the files from your parents' deaths and your assault. Why would he be interested in them?"

"How would I know? Ask him." What was I besides surprised? A mind reader?

"Now don't get snappy. What the hell is going on out there in New Hampshire? Is he trying to figure out where Jeremy Bronson is or are you in trouble?"

"Again, I think you should discuss the matter with him and not me. I haven't seen Kilbride lately. He doesn't share his theories. Why he's interested in Jeremy Bronson, or the death of my parents, is of no consequence to me."

"We're still searching for Bronson. He'll pay for what he's done."

"Right. Now if that's all?" I held in a breath and waited for him to disconnect. When he didn't hang up, I sensed hesitation and asked, "Is there something else, Detective?"

"No, no, nothing." He grew silent again. Seconds passed. "If you must know, this detective of yours has a history in New York City. He was involved with a shooting that resulted in a woman being killed. Were you aware of that?"

"He's not *my detective*. I don't care about him or his history. I must get back to work." Before Brent could speak, I hit the end button, slammed the phone into the charger, and listened to the silence surrounding me. If I could manage to get my nerves and heartbeat to match the peace and serenity in the room, I'd be fine.

The bell jingled when the studio door opened. I swung to face Kilbride as he strode in. When I saw the expression on his face, my day grew dim, as did my sense of gloom. I tossed the pen aside and draped the rendering with a white cloth.

"Nice work," he said just before I secured the cover in place.

"I'm sure you didn't come by to admire my artwork, Kilbride."

His blue gaze seemed to drink me in. My pulse rate hiked alarmingly. I knew, if he touched me, I couldn't be trusted to leave his clothes and body intact.

A warning went off in my head as Detective Brent's phone call echoed in my ears.

Was Jonah up to no good, or was he sincerely interested in finding Bronson? And if so why? Doubts overshadowed my lust as insecurity cast its spell over me.

His hands went up to ward of any chance of an attack, verbal or physical, and Kilbride said, "I thought you might help me."

Without interest, I answered him. "In what way?"

"When you were in Flora's house, did you consider odd places where she might hide a journal or diary? It's an old house, built before the turn of the century when safes weren't popular. I'm thinking built-in private storage might be a perspective I need to consider."

Surprised by how apropos his question was, I wondered if Gretchen had spoken to him. Unwilling to ask, I said, "My grandparents had a vacation house like that. Exploring hidden spaces as a child appealed to my creative nature, and filled rainy days with mystery. The fireplace and bookcases, especially, were unique. There was storage behind a side panel of the fireplace, and the bookcase had a narrow hidden room behind it. My grandfather showed me where it lay, secreted away. The house was part of the historic and notorious underground railroad."

His eyes alight, Jonah stepped closer, drew a stool from beneath the work table, and plunked his butt on it. "If Flora had such a space, where would it be? I wonder ..."

The phone interrupted his words. When I answered, Gretchen was on the line.

"Is tonight good for you to return the journals? I'm free at seven o'clock. My last appointment is a haircut at five-thirty."

"Sure."

"Is something wrong?" she asked.

"Not at all, Detective Kilbride just came in with a theory."

"Did you give him the journals?" Gretchen whispered into the phone.

"He wondered if there's a secret panel or such in Flora's house. Have you heard of one at Flora's, Gretch?" I asked, my eyes locked on Jonah's face. I gave a headshake.

"Gotcha, I'll see you at seven. My place. Be punctual."

"Okay, bye."

His eyes narrowed, Jonah regarded me in silence. I set the phone aside and returned my attention to him.

"She said she's unaware of Flora's house particulars. Sorry. You could check them yourself, though. Town Hall or the building inspector's office must have floor plans of all Schmitz Landing homes. If the measurements don't match the interior walls, then you'll likely find what you're looking for." I shrugged. "Wish I could be more helpful."

Yeah, what a crock of crap. I lied through my teeth and was sure to be arrested for interfering with an investigation — and probably for breaking and entering. At any rate, my road to hell was clearly paved.

He nodded and slid from the stool. His radio sounded. He mumbled into the speaker and then offered me his thanks. Before he left, Jonah smiled, ran a finger along my cheek, and leaned in to brush the area with his lips. My heart raced, my blood boiled, and I stepped into him, drawing his face closer to mine. We locked lips, I pushed against him and went for the gold medal.

"I want you," I breathed against his lips.

His rich blue eyes, filled with heat, gazed into mine as he gently put me away from him.

"I can't." He turned and left me standing alone, feeling stupid and embarrassed.

Chapter 15

TIME SLOWED TO a standstill, or so it seemed, while I waited to meet Gretchen. I'd cleaned the house, vacuumed carpets and floors, collected dust-bunnies from under the bed, washed laundry, and fought off thoughts of Jonah Kilbride.

When the clock hands reached ten minutes to seven, I reached for a dark windbreaker, tossed cat crunchies in Jasmine's bowl, and left her with a promise to return soon. Flora's journals were tucked safely at the bottom of my canvas carryall. I'd stuffed a package of fresh rolls, and some lunch meats accompanied by fresh fruit, on top of them. If Jonah should come along and ask what was in the bag, I'd answer with proof that Gretchen and I were meeting up for a light repast. My trip to hell loomed closer.

Taking her stairs two at a time, I reached her apartment as Gretchen opened the door and greeted me. Her eyes held a warning.

"Oh, good, you're here." She waved me inside.

I stared at her, all the while wondering why she appeared panic ridden. My gaze landed on the back of a familiar head and I caught my breath.

"Jonah, what are you doing here?"

"Waiting for you. Gretchen was good enough to share info about Flora's background, the gossip she's heard — including some history of the town. Wasn't that nice of her? So, what's in the bag?"

It was apparent he'd heard more of our phone conversation than I wanted him to. Keen ears and eyes were part and parcel of his makeup. *Geez, Louise.*

I handed the rolls, fruit, and meats to Gretchen and lowered the bag to the floor behind the sofa.

"Just supper. Care to join us?" I answered with what I hoped was a charming smile.

"No, no, I can't stay. Enjoy your meal. I'll catch you later." His smile widened. Would he catch us later? Was he saying he'd stop by to see me later that night? I figured he meant the former rather than the latter.

To be sure he was gone, Gretchen and I waited until Kilbride's car disappeared from view. Then we scooted down the rear staircase of Gretchen's building. Her backyard consisted of a few trash receptacles, lawn chairs strewn haphazardly along chain link fencing, a dilapidated gas grill, and a mixture of colored pots filled with sad-looking artificial flowers that had seen better times.

I slanted a look at Gretchen and she shrugged. "The bakery owners, Jeff and Jill, have their lunch out here in good weather. The tacky flowers and ugly pots are Jill's way of making the area cheery." Her eyebrows lifted as did one shoulder giving her a comical air. I chuckled.

Wending our way through back lots of other shops on the street, I noted most shop owners were fanatical about the way their storefronts and backyards appeared. I was impressed by the neatness of it all.

We'd reached Flora's street before I realized where we were. Darkness had descended and we whispered to one another about how and where to break into the house. I rounded a corner of the building and saw the rotted frame of a cellar window that dangled by one hinge. The window was an old affair, much like the house. I knew I'd fit, but being big-boned, Gretchen wouldn't. I whispered, "I'll go inside. You hold onto the bag of journals. I'll let you in through the door."

In agreement, Gretchen took the bag, slung it to the ground behind her, and helped me pry off the rotted frame using flat-head screwdrivers she'd brought. After a brief bit of digging and prying, the window broke away, leaving splintered wood shards behind. I stuck my flashlight into the dark opening while Gretchen set the window aside. The drop to the basement floor looked no more than six feet at most.

"Take my hands to steady me as I go down," I instructed Gretchen.

I turned onto my stomach, stuck my legs through the opening and wiggled backwards through the opening while Gretchen held my hands in a tight grip. As I slid down, I called, "Okay, let go."

I hit the floor with a thump.

I fell backward, stumbled, and landed on my backside. My flashlight flew from my pocket, hit the floor, and clattered into darkness. I was feeling around for it when Gretchen shined her light through the gap.

"Are you all right?"

"I can't find my flashlight."

She swung a beam of light to and fro. I caught a glimpse of it where it had lodged against the furnace. Skittering sounds sent a chill along my spine. I snatched the flashlight and scrambled to my feet, hastily backing away for fear of being attacked by rodents.

"I'll meet you around the side of the house," I called in a soft voice.

"Sure thing."

I stumbled up the short flight of stairs and opened the door into the house proper. I entered a hallway at the furthest end of the house and made my way to the side door, swinging the beam of light to and fro as I went.

Gretchen rushed inside once I opened the door for her. Chilled to the bone, she shook off the cold, handed me the bag, and rubbed her hands together.

"It still gets cold at night in April. Gosh, I'm freezing. Let's get this over with."

We rushed to the second floor bedroom, opened the secret panel, and Gretchen shoved the journals inside. I stuffed the bag into my jacket pocket. We froze when the downstairs door opened and heavy footsteps sounded on the stairs.

"Shut the flashlight off," I whispered. I pressed the panel and heard it click in place, grabbed Gretchen, dragged her into the corner closet, leaving the door slightly ajar. Our sneakers were silent on the carpeted floor, and I sent a silent word of thanks to anyone who might be listening.

We blinked through the thin opening as bright light blazed, illuminating the entire room. It seemed nobody had ordered discontinuation of the electricity. Kilbride sauntered into view, his gaze on the fireplace as he stood before it. He pressed, pushed, and finally swore at the hard surface when it refused to cooperate.

Jonah ran a hand across his cropped hair and peered closer. He focused on the surrounding trim. He twisted and turned until he gained access to the stash of journals.

"Ah, this is where she hid them." Jonah whistled as he flipped through the pages. "You can come out now," he called to us.

Silent, we held our breath and waited. I slid a glance to Gretchen when the door flew open and we were dragged from within the confined space by our jacket collars, both of us shocked and blithering words of denial.

Hands on his hips, Jonah demanded, "What do you think you're doing? Didn't I say I'd arrest you if I caught you two here again?"

We stepped back in unison and began explaining ourselves at the same time. He put a hand up and we fell silent. He pointed to Gretchen. "You, go ahead."

She told him we wanted to help his investigation by trying to find a place where the diary or journal he sought might be hidden. She said we only had his best interests at heart. I could see by his expression that he thought her a poor liar. The entire time she spoke, my head bobbed up and down in bobble doll fashion.

His cold blue-eyed stare landed on me. "Is that true? Don't

lie, or I swear, I'll lock you both up for the night. And before you get brave and say you're not scared of me, consider this Katarina ... You should be."

I could tell he would brook no foolishness and said, soft-voiced, "She's telling the truth. We only wanted to help." I am *such* a liar. Call it survival, or whatever, but I was determined to stay out of jail, out of trouble, and to keep our stories the same. No rats-leaving-a-ship here.

He nodded, though his eyes showed he didn't believe either of us. He retrieved the journals from the mantel and said, "If these are hers, they could tell me what dirt Flora had on everyone. I'd like to know who attempted to kill Janet and if she was attacked in order to keep their secret safe. Maybe these will reveal all."

I leaned forward to look at the books in his hand and realized there were only two. I glanced into the compartment again. Nothing there. One of the three must have gotten stuck in the back of my closet. Dang. I'd been in such a rush to relieve myself of their presence, I hadn't counted them. Unwilling to admit to a missing journal, I agreed the information within their pages might solve the mystery.

Jonah herded us down the stairs, out the door, and into his car. He drove to Gretchen's apartment with an order to get out. Single file, all three of us climbed the stairs. I had a wicked sense of foreboding, but couldn't think of any way to escape from our present dilemma.

Gretchen opened her apartment door and motioned us inside. I flopped on the sofa and Gretchen set coffee to perk. Jonah settled in an armchair, his long legs stretched out, his feet crossed at the ankles. He studied me, his eyes sparkling with anger. I plucked at the lace on my sneaker and avoided his glare.

From the kitchen, Gretchen called, "Who wants a sandwich? I'm freakin' starving."

"Sounds like a good idea," I said and swung a look to Jonah who nodded and stood up to join us in the neat room.

We'd eaten our way through a few sandwiches and the

fruit I'd brought when Gretchen passed around the pastry she'd bought from the bakery after work.

"I thought we might need sustenance after our search of Flora's house, so I purchased these." She handed apple walnut brownies to us. A light sugar glaze smothered the top of the delightful tasty treats.

"Now, tell me the truth," Jonah said to Gretchen. "Were you aware of Flora's hiding place, or were you guessing?"

"I'd heard she had written things about people. You know, as a hairdresser, you hear lots of stuff, some true and some not, but I'd never given it much thought. When Katie mentioned you wondered if there were such places in Flora's house, I got to thinking."

"Well, the next time you have a thought such as that, call me — not Katie. There's a killer on the loose in this town. Flora's been killed, Janet was attacked and could have died, and you both could have been in serious trouble if it hadn't been me in Flora's house tonight." Jonah turned to me and said, "You'll need to put the window back in place, by the way."

Startled, I asked, "H-how did you know?"

He interrupted me with a laugh. "I walked the perimeter of the house before entering. I found the grass mashed flat, the window nearby, and most certainly knew you two were inside. I really ought to arrest you both."

"You can't do that. We just fed you," Gretchen whined.

I reached out and touched her shoulder. "Gretch, you sound ridiculous. He can, but probably won't arrest us, okay?"

His eyebrows lifted. Jonah's cynical expression increased my pulse rate. "You're sure of that, are you, Katarina?"

Fear. Such an unrewarding feeling. I hadn't felt fear in ages, and while I wasn't exactly fearful now, I can admit to discomfort. I held his gaze in silence.

Gretchen looked at us in turn. "What's with the Katarina thing? Did I miss something?"

Jonah chortled and rose from the chair. "I'll be around. Don't break and enter again ladies, or I *will* arrest you. Be sure of it." He strode across the room, glanced at us from the doorway, and then his footsteps rumbled like thunder down the stairs.

We waited until he started his car before creeping to the windows to peep through the curtains. Jonah drove off in the direction of the police station. I turned to Gretchen, huffed a huge sigh, plopped on the sofa, and ruffled my hair with my fingertips.

"He's got it bad for you, Katie. You know that, right?"

I coughed. "No, he doesn't. He thinks I know more about the murders, and he's trying to figure out how to get me to talk. Unfortunately for him, I haven't any information, and I don't want any either."

"What's with the name?" Gretchen insisted.

I shrugged. "My given name is Katarina, not Katie. He knows I don't like the name, so he calls me Katarina to annoy me."

She pushed the subject. "Sounds like love to me."

I pushed back. "There's no love there, just his job. Believe me, I know that all too well." I bit my lip before I said another word. Gretchen's eyes narrowed and she stared at me for a second, but didn't ask the question I knew was eating at her. She wanted me to explain how I knew he loved his job more than anything.

I bounded from the sofa, stated I had to leave, and without waiting for her to utter another word, scooted out the door. The brisk walk home cleared my head. I thought of Janet, Flora, and Jonah. Janet had been in the alley when she was jumped from behind. Jonah had told me she'd never seen her assailant, but I figured she must have known something that got her attacked. It was time to read the last journal.

Met at the door by Jasmine, I set the house alarm before hanging up my coat. The cat wound around my feet and legs as I walked toward the back of the house, her meowing loud and demanding. I guess I'd been gone too long for her liking. I reached down and scratched her ears.

"She's good company for you." Jonah's soft voice filtered through the room. I jumped at the sound.

"What do you want?" I demanded. "And, how did you get in?"

"You left the kitchen door unlocked, very unsafe I might add." He shook his head in admonishment at my lack of precautions for personal safety. "I figured you'd be home soon. Gretchen asked about the name, am I right?" His laughter matched the softness of his voice. He'd been sitting next to the fireplace but rose and approached me when I entered the cozy room.

"She did. I offered a brief answer and beat feet out of there. She's too inquisitive. Now answer my question, what do you want?"

"That's a leading question. We both know what I want, but can't have, so let's head in the other direction. What do you know that you're not sharing?"

We'd been over this old ground before. It had become annoying. I ran my fingers along the mantel edge and looked him in the face. "I might ask the same question. Why did you ask for the Bronson files?"

"Ah, the good detective's been in touch with you." Jonah shrugged. "I thought a fresh pair of eyes might offer insight as to where Bronson might have gone. If I can eliminate him from your life, maybe you'll find peace."

"By eliminate, you mean imprison?"

He laughed an honest-to-goodness deep sound that made me smile.

He dipped his head and confirmed, "Yes, imprison. I don't go around killing people."

"So what do you think I'm hiding from you?" I asked as I snuggled into an armchair.

He resumed his seat, lifted a journal, and wobbled it back and forth. "Flora kept more dirt on the residents in this town than God is probably aware of. Some might be true, but some is pure tripe. Her ability to turn words to her own advantage would make talk show history if she were still alive. Even *60 Minutes* would want to interview her."

I grinned at the assumption while picturing the *60 Minutes'* crew. After a glance at the book, I looked at his expression. He found her words as distasteful as I had. Somehow that comforted me.

"Good reading, is it?" I wanted him to affirm my suspicions.

"Awful stuff. A deranged woman, that's what she was." Jonah tossed the journal aside. "Paranoid and rotten to the core. It's a wonder she hadn't been murdered long ago. I'm curious as to why she was left on your bench, though, and why somebody would use the same style of murder weapon with the attempt on Janet Latchkey. The killer had been confident he'd be able to kill Janet. He must have been shocked when he wasn't able to. Any ideas on who would attack her?"

"None. I've given it a lot of thought. You're probably correct in your assumption that Janet was expected to keel over and die. Good thing she'd taken a few self-preservation lessons. She called you about the sweet smell, right?"

"Yes, I'm not sure what it means, but I think it could be important. Would you read the journals?" Jonah asked, offering them to me.

"I'd rather not." A sudden chill hit me. "Negativity breeds the same. If Flora's words are as bad as you say, then I don't wish to read them." I certainly wasn't about to admit to having scanned them before I hid them in the mantel's compartment.

He slapped the books together and settled against the back of the chair once more. "You're smart to avoid involvement in her shady business. Sorry I asked. I thought you might see them from a different viewpoint than I have."

Not about to embark on that trail, I shook my head and again refused his request. I did plan to read the last one that was still upstairs, though. Then I'd have to decide how to turn it over to Jonah without him having a snit fit. Lies ... They add up and become a heavy burden, like carrying a load of logs on your shoulders. It was too much to bear, even for those used to carrying them.

My guilt rode me, leaving my spirit deflated. Tired of the

whole situation, I rose, turned off the alarm, asked Jonah to let himself out, and started up the stairs. Halfway to the second floor, I heard the lock click as it took hold. Jonah was gone. Jasmine and I were alone. I breathed a hefty sigh of relief.

Cold and weary, I showered, slipped my pajamas on, and shuffled the bedcovers down. Jasmine cuddled nearby. I pulled the comforter over my body and flipped open the first page of the last journal. I read on and on until my vision blurred.

Unaware of falling asleep, I awoke to a few remembered fragments of a dream concerning Jill Crantz, the baker's wife, and Ray Jenkins. My mind muddled — the dream made no sense. I swept the bedding to the floor, stretched, yawned, and tried to revisit the dream one step at a time.

They embraced, kissing passionately. Ray's face filled with pleasure. He drew back and stared into Jill's eyes. His expression turned to one of horror as Jill became Flora Middly. I shook my head to clear the memories of the dream. It was yet another kind of nightmare.

The students would arrive soon and I'd overslept. I shook off the dream and readied for the day.

Chapter 16

MUSICAL NOTES RANG each time the studio door opened. The bell had gotten a workout, what with students arriving and leaving, the local committee chairwoman asking for my participation in the spring program run by Schmitz Landing's historical folks, and finally, a visit from Ray Jenkins asking me to place an ad in the newspaper.

My present work of art stood untouched on the easel behind me. Shrouded by cloth, it silently beckoned. As often as I'd tried to summon the energy and free time to complete the illustration, I couldn't manage to finish it.

Interruptions are dangerous for artists. We find all sorts of reasons to avoid our projects without having others interfere with our time as well. I glanced at the easel and faced Ray as he settled at the work table across from me. I held my breath, counted to ten, and then gave him my full attention. I'd have to apply myself to the artwork later.

"It's nice to see you. What can I do for you, Ray?"

Ray placed his folder on the work table, flipped open the cover, and shuffled the pages within. He glanced at the first sheet, looked at me, and then blurted out that though he hated to ask, his boss was forcing him to go door-to-door asking for advertising for the *Schmitz Landing Daily*. His face turned beet red. I couldn't figure out if he was embarrassed or angry or both.

"Let's see what you have to offer." I leaned forward to get a look at the ad sizes as Ray slipped the paper toward me. I perused the ads and costs then agreed to place a few in the upcoming month in the Sunday issues.

A smile spread across his face as Ray put the papers back in order. "Would you like me to work up the package for you with graphics and all, like the last time?"

I agreed since he was good at that part of the job. "That would be great. If you'd email them to me, I'll let you know if they're good to go."

"Sure thing." Ray hesitated and said, "I heard Kilbride found some journals at Flora's house."

"W-where did you hear that?" I stammered.

There was a gleam in his eyes as Ray warmed to the subject. "I have my sources. You realize as a newspaper man, I can't reveal that information to you. Let's suffice it to say I know it's the truth. Why, just yesterday, Kilbride came to see me at the newspaper. He asked questions about Janet's attack, Flora's murder, you, and others in town." His lips turned up a bit at the corners, but his eyes glittered with malice. Slowly, he murmured, "I can't imagine what he thought I could tell him about you."

Alarmed, I asked, "He asked about me? What did he want to know?"

Ray stopped fiddling with the dog-eared corner of the folder and stared at me. My breath caught in my throat. The snide smirk on his face didn't bode well.

Nonchalantly, he flicked a hand and answered. "I guess he was curious about the slaying of your family in Ohio. That's what happened, right? They were supposedly slain by your old boyfriend?"

Still as a deer in the headlights, I wondered if my heart had indeed leapt from my chest or ceased beating at the revelation he'd made. How did he know? When had he found out? What else was he aware of? Would he expose me to his readers? Had he told Jonah or had Jonah told him? Thoughts tumbled through my mind as fast as a boulder tumbling over a cliff.

My voice so soft, I whispered, "I don't know what you're talking about."

From the bottom page of the file, Ray pulled a picture of me being taken into custody by Columbus police detectives. The caption read: Famous artist questioned in the brutal murder of parents.

I cringed. I'd been hounded by the police for weeks during my hospital stay. The medical staff had refused to allow the police to see me due to the severity of my injuries. Still, the police had waited impatiently, stubbornly, and with a growing sense of anger at having been put off. The day I'd arrived home to finish my recovery, Detective Brent had marched me to the station to begin his interrogation with an intensity that shocked and scared the crap out of me. I'd never forget it.

That experience was burned into my psyche. Detective Brent could never say '*I'm sorry*' often enough to remove the horrific and terrifying memories of his cruelty. I shifted in the chair, studied the picture, and glanced at Ray.

"Where did you get this?"

He smirked and withdrew a sheaf of papers from the folder. He flipped each page across the table toward me with a tick of his fingertips.

"When you moved to Schmitz Landing, I sensed there was more to you than met the eye. Flora was all over your art, and you were too sweet to be true. I wondered why you came to this go-nowhere, be-nothing, tourist town. By your bearing and artwork alone, I knew you were something special. I did some digging. It took a while, but I found what I was looking for. Did you kill your parents, Katie, or should I say Katarina? Or was it really your old boyfriend?"

Where had this new and horrid Ray Jenkins sprung from? I'd never seen this side of him, or maybe I just hadn't wanted to acknowledge it. The town, its residents, the location, all of it had appeared ideal when I first arrived. It had seemed a magical fairytale town, something out of the *Heidi* story.

I frowned at the sheets of paper, each with pictures of me escorted by various lawmen, my lawyer, and finally one of me at the funeral of my parents, placing flowers on their caskets. I glanced at the picture of me and my attorney. My backbone stiffened and I sat up straight.

I slid the papers back toward Ray and felt my anger grow as I stared at him. "Why have you brought these here now?"

"I wanted to see your face when I said that you'll be my next feature story." He grinned. "You've been reading my features, haven't you?"

"Yes." As hard as it was, I admitted, "I thought each one was better than the last. Why would you want to publish something as painful for me as an article featuring this when you could expand on the studio and its students, the gallery and shows, how the art of tangling has benefits for those who are in need and the like?"

"People enjoy gritty news. They like dirt, and they have a right to know. It's my job to bring them news and you are newsworthy, Katie." His self-satisfaction apparent, Ray nearly rubbed his hands together with glee at the thought of revealing my horror story to all.

I hadn't found peace after all. When this news broke, my small-town life would be over. I'd have to move on and start again. Maybe I'd become a hermit. The idea appealed to me. Then anger took over and elbowed my self-pity aside. *Get a grip Katie, haven't you been through enough? Stand up for yourself. Tell him to stuff it.*

I leaned forward, placed my elbows on the table and flattened my hands on the surface. "If you think it's necessary to drag me through the mud, forcing me to relive a situation not of my making, but one that nearly ruined my life, then go ahead. I must warn you, Ray, I have a team of really good lawyers who will take you apart. If you aren't already aware of it, I'll outline a few things for you.

"I'm wealthy, and have been for years. Money has never been an issue for me, not even before my parents died." I pointed to the town beyond my studio windows. "I live and work here because I adore this town. I was famous for my unique artwork. I got mixed up with a man who turned out to be a killer. He took my parents from me and then tried to finish me off as well." I stretched the neck of my sweater downward so he could see a scar or two. "After what I've been through, if you think that you can casually trash me in your newspaper while trying to make a name for yourself, you'd better reconsider. I won't stand for it, do you hear me? I'll sue you and the newspaper if you print a word."

By this time, my voice had risen, and I'd thumped my fist on the table. Jasmine stood at attention a foot away from Ray, her ears twitching, her claws at the ready, a nasty gleam in her eyes.

Ray's skin reddened. He swept up the papers and folder and shuffled them in order. His composure still in place, he spoke with confidence. "I'll consider not running the story. I won't promise anything. You're big news that could put me on the map. Even Flora knew you had something to hide. She asked me time and again if I knew what you were all about. I denied knowing. The story was mine to tell, not hers to blackmail you with."

"Blackmail? Flora blackmailed people?"

"Didn't you realize Flora made her living off others' infidelity, mistakes, and the like? She didn't have a job, her family wasn't well-off, and she certainly wasn't likeable."

Thinking hard, I mumbled, "I hadn't considered her a blackmailer, but it makes sense. She never tried to blackmail me, thanks to you, but she managed to intimate she had knowledge of me that others would enjoy hearing." I sighed. "I didn't give her insinuations much credence since I figured I'd done a good job of covering my background."

"As far as I know, Flora knew nothing concrete, but she sure could smell a secret."

"Hmm. Well, about *good* journalism ... It isn't about trashing the lives of others. It's all about reporting important matters, telling good stories ... To be honest, I would rather read a heartwarming story than read the garbage that's out there now. You're talented, Ray, you really are. Don't sell yourself short for a job at the big newspapers. It isn't as much fun there as you think it is." Staring into his still-red face, I was unsure if my advice sank in, so I continued, "In Schmitz Landing you get to tell everyone information that's important to them, the stuff that makes them want to read the paper every day. Am I right?"

Ray pulled the pictures from the folder, stared at them for a moment, and tucked them away. Maybe I'd won the battle, but I wasn't sure about the war.

"You may right. I'll think about what you've said." He closed the folder, tucked it beneath his arm, and glanced at me. "You're lucky Flora didn't find out. She'd have taunted you before spreading it around town like a wildfire out of control. The woman was evil."

"I know. She was mean and insensitive at best." I rubbed my brows and said, "I'd appreciate your keeping my past to yourself. Please consider how hard I've worked to start a new life after a tragic past"

He dipped his head.

"The other thing you might consider is, the man who killed my parents is still at large. I don't need him hunting me down. If you run the story, he might see it. That would bring a whole new perspective to my life."

His eyes widened. In light of his earlier attitude, I wasn't sure I bought his turn about.

"I hadn't thought of that, but I'll keep it in mind."

"That's all I ask."

Even though I felt uncomfortable with the knowledge that anyone other than Kilbride knew my backstory, I prayed Ray wouldn't run with the story.

Ray walked from the building and hastened across the green toward his office. I watched from the window until he disappeared from view, then turned to Jasmine.

"That was a close one, Jasmine. Too close for comfort."

I removed the trash bag from the basket then tied it tight and tossed it into the bin behind the house. While outside, I took a moment to appreciate the view to the river and beyond. Leaves had turned green, grass sprouted, and the drab winter was no longer present. I breathed in lungs full of fresh air, took a last look around, and headed inside to finish the illustration.

While I worked, Ray's conversation returned and ran like a damaged video in my head. It kept catching at the statement Ray had made about Flora finding out about me. When the pen slipped for the fourth time, I stepped back, threw it on the table, and loudly complained about my lack of concentration.

I'd just draped the work with its cloth when the doorbell chimed. In a huff, I swung about to see who'd be next to ruin my day. As if Ray's visit wasn't enough, Jonah stood in the doorway, his face a mask of distrust. *Now what?*

"Don't stand there with the door wide open, come on in." I beckoned him with my fingers and watched as he complied.

"Got any coffee?" he asked with a grimace.

Oh my, this wasn't good. I nodded and led him to the kitchen, gestured to a chair, and set about making a fresh pot of brew.

Chapter 17

"WHAT'S ON YOUR mind?" I asked, but was sure I didn't want to know. With the kitchen sink at my back, I leaned against it and waited for him to talk about whatever caused his foul mood.

"I've gone over the file I received from your good friend Brent. For what it's worth, the only possible answer as to where Bronson went after his killing spree is to jail. Whether it's here in the States or in Mexico or Canada, he's got to be in the can. Brent searched for the man using every possible angle he could think of — some I hadn't even thought of — and he couldn't find Bronson anywhere."

I'd hoped for better news. If Bronson were in jail, why hadn't he shown up somewhere? His name would have been noted in a national database, wouldn't it? Heck, even I knew about such things. After all, I watch *CSI* and *NCIS* on television, so why wouldn't Bronson's name have shown up?

After serving coffee and sitting in a chair across from Jonah, I sipped coffee and considered how my past was still in my present. Annoying as it was, I couldn't escape.

"Is there a way to find out if he's imprisoned in Mexico? I know the federals there don't like Americans sticking their noses in Mexican business, but if you go through official sources, maybe you could find out?"

"Great minds, Katarina, great minds." Jonah laughed and slurped a mouthful of coffee. Jasmine leapt to his lap and gazed at me over the edge of the table. It was almost as if she grinned at me.

Jonah smacked his lips, offered his cup for more coffee, and said, "I called a friend of mine at FBI headquarters in New York who's worked with the Mexican authorities. He's going to see what he can find out and call me. Let's hope he has good news. I checked prisons in this country. He's not locked up here."

"I could use some good news right about now."

An eyebrow shot upward, Jonah's eyes took on an interested gleam, and he asked, "Something happen I should know about?"

I gave him a quick rundown of my conversation with Ray Jenkins and watched his face when I said Ray had mentioned Jonah's questions about me.

"Why would you ask Ray questions about me? You know all there is to know." I fiddled with the coffee cup handle and waited for an explanation.

"I didn't question Ray. Actually, I haven't seen the guy in about a week or so. When I did, it was just in passing at the café."

"So, you never went to his office yesterday?"

Tapping the raised scar next to his eye, Jonah said, "No, I didn't. It's curious he'd say that."

"He acted weird. One minute he asked for an ad placement, the next he threatened to publish my background so he could make headlines and move on to a larger newspaper. I lost my temper, threatened him with a lawsuit, and then calmed down enough to explain how it would spoil my life here, and that Bronson might still be at large — and that might prove detrimental to my health should Bronson get wind of the story and find me."

Jasmine perked up when my voice rose as I repeated what happened. I reached across the table and scratched her forehead as she peered over the edge. I chuckled and mentioned Jasmine's reaction to my anger, including her readiness to protect me from Ray.

Jonah laughed, stroked her fur, and smoothed her ears with his fingertips. Jasmine purred. She rubbed her face against his hand, enjoying the attention.

"She's very protective, you have a good friend." Jonah

grinned as Jasmine curled into his lap.

"Indeed. I wished she'd been there when Bronson did his handiwork, she'd have shown him a thing or two." I chuckled, even though it wasn't a joke. Where could the man be hiding?

Reluctant to know if he had read them, I asked Jonah, "Have you finished reading Flora's journals?"

"I got through the first one and am halfway into the other. It's hard to read the ranting of a sick person." He shook his head, a bleak look on his face.

I remembered what Ray had said. "Oh, Ray mentioned it was a good thing Flora didn't know about me because she would have tried to blackmail me. I thought that interesting, don't you? Did she mention blackmail in her journals?"

Surprise splashed across Jonah's face.

"Not so far. It's an aspect I hadn't really considered. Now that you mention it, Flora wasn't employed anywhere. I'd assumed she lived on family money or such. The journal I have now ends around a year or so ago. Maybe there's another journal that she hid elsewhere. I should look again."

"Mmm," I said and left it at that. I hadn't gotten a third of the way through the journal upstairs, but now realized I needed to get on with it. Then I'd turn it over to Jonah. He'd be angry, but I'd faced that before and would handle it.

He glanced at the wall clock behind me and asked if I'd like to have dinner at the café. Knowing the fresh air would do me good along with a decent meal, I agreed to go, insisting we walk the green to get there.

We passed benches overshadowed by trees with foliage that offered blissful shade during summer months. Jonah noted the beauty of spring in New Hampshire.

Wondering aloud, I asked, "Have you any leads on Janet's assault?"

Jonah's face took on a somber expression as he peered down at me. "No, it's clear she wasn't expecting it. I've questioned her a few times, hoping she remembered hearing gossip that may have sparked the attempt on her life. So far, she hasn't admitted to knowing anything. I'm frustrated by the lack of evidence or clues. There weren't any fingerprints on the belt, either. It was decorated the same as the one before."

"Janet's a good person who deserved better that what she got, Jonah. Maybe I can try jogging her memory."

"True enough. If you'd like to give her a try, go ahead."

He opened the café door and waited for me to precede him. Ah, chivalry. I grinned and headed toward a booth. We'd scanned the menus given to us by the waitress who brought place settings and tried to chat us up.

"I'm Melanie and I'll be your server. If you need anything, just let me know." She began to walk away, hesitated, and then returned to us.

"You're the woman who owns the studio across the green, right?" Melanie asked.

The short chubby woman of around thirty-five had an inquisitive gleam in her eyes and a cheerful smile on her face.

"Yes, I am." I lifted my hand to shake hers and introduced myself.

Before I could say a word, she announced, "I've a piece of your work from years ago, when you had a gallery show in Chicago."

Stricken, I gaped, tried to quickly recover and pasted a smile on my face. "Do you? Which one, exactly?"

Melanie warmed to the subject. "I have the one named *Cru-da-tay*. Do you remember that one? It's in my living room. It's quite a large illustration."

The smile on my face stiffened as I thought back to the day I had sold it. My agent had called and said he had buyers for several works. I was excited and had asked him to ship them immediately. That was the same day my parents lost their lives.

"I'm glad you're enjoying it. I don't often have the opportunity to meet an owner." I glanced at Jonah. My mouth dried like desert sand. I sipped my glass of water and considered the fact that the waitress remembered me.

Jonah handed the menus to Melanie and said we were all

set. She nodded, took our order, and said she'd be right back. I slumped as she walked away. My day had taken a downturn and was headed into the crapper. First Ray's stunning revelation, then Jonah's news he hadn't found Jeremy Bronson, and now an art lover from my past … Could things get any worse?

The café, a hub of activity at the best of times, became busier and busier. Warm weather brought people out, reviving them after the long months of winter. I watched Melanie scoot from table to table, a coffee pot in her hand and menus bunched in the crook of her arm. Where was Janet tonight?

Melanie smiled and quickly placed our dinners in front of us. Before she rushed off to the next booth, I asked after Janet and was told she had the night off. With a nod, I watched Melanie hurry away and grinned at Jonah.

"Let's hope our waitress doesn't have time to stop by for another conversation," I said.

Jonah assured me he'd intercept her, if possible. I smiled and finished the last of my dinner.

After leaving the cafe, we walked the town, set out in a square format where shops sat opposite the green. Delightful as Schmitz Landing was, I had a sense that I'd never again feel as I did the first time I drove into town, when I'd instantly fallen in love with it. Too much had happened recently that skewed that view.

Jonah folded my hand in his as we ambled across the green. I turned to stare at the café, picturing Janet's assault. How had the criminal managed to leave the dead end alley without being seen?

"What did Janet say about the mishap?" I asked Jonah.

"It was hardly a mishap." Jonah slid a sideways half-grin at me. "She hadn't seen anyone lurking, but hadn't been looking for him or her, either. When she was found by her co-worker, the perp had already disappeared. Neither of them have a clue as to who could have done it. When I asked Janet how tall she thought the person was, she realized her attacker was shorter than her. I'd say Janet stands around five-foot-seven. That means a person who wanted to strangle her would be shorter, but they'd need to be tall enough to swing the belt over Janet's head and drag her downward to get a tight grip. Someone who's not too short, and with enough strength to manage a person of Janet's size. Why? What are you thinking?"

Something niggled at me, but I couldn't figure out what. "She's taller than I am. Maybe she'd allow me to play out the scene with her. That way we might spark a memory she isn't aware of now." I rubbed my face, yawned, and said, "I can't figure out what's bothering me about the whole thing. I'm sure it'll surface sooner or later."

Jonah nodded and halted as I gazed at the buildings that surrounded the green. "Let's come back around ten tonight," I said, "and see whose lights are on and whose aren't. That might offer some insight on who may have seen something, who didn't want to become involved, or who just discarded the sight as unimportant. There are apartments above many of the businesses directly surrounding this park. Gretchen's is over there." I pointed to the bakery. "Though the trees might block the view of the cafe."

"Good idea. We'll revisit the scene later, after dark. While I walk one side of the park and you walk the other, we can check the lights to see who's up and who isn't."

We'd reached Tangled Wings by then and traipsed the driveway toward the kitchen door. I'd left lights on and saw Jasmine at the window over the sink, peering into the night. She scratched at the glass with one paw as we topped the stairs.

"Guess your friend is glad you're home." Jonah chuckled.

"It's nice to be greeted when I get home," I admitted. "Are you coming in?"

"There are things back at the station that I should check on. I'll come by for you when the café closes, okay?"

"Fine, see you then." I smiled, thanked him for dinner, and greeted Jasmine.

Chapter 18

THE CLOCK HANDS dragged. While I waited to meet Jonah, I opened Flora's journal. Her wicked stories and appalling remarks concerning those who crossed her path were disturbing. I'd gotten three-quarters into the book when the clock chimed. I'd be late if I didn't get going.

From the front window, I thought I saw Jonah's car at the curb. Thinking that maybe he'd gone into the park without me, I zipped a jacket over my sweater and raced across the street onto the green. Paying no attention to where I was headed, or to sounds that surrounded me, I was unprepared for what happened.

I tripped, flew headlong, and sprawled onto the path. *Oomph.* Hauling in a deep breath, I sat up, peered at what had caused my fall ... and crab-like, I backed away on all fours. A body lay crumpled on the ground, covered in the darkness of heavy shadows from the enormous trees bordering the path. I glanced around, taking in my surroundings for fear a perp still hid within dark areas where street and park lights didn't reach. Street noise was slight. Most people had turned in for the night, shops were locked up tight, hardly any cars were on the street, and I was alone with a body. Where was Jonah? *Was the body Jonah's?*

I scrambled closer to see who I'd tripped over. Without touching it, I peaked at the inert form. It certainly wasn't Jonah. The body wasn't large or rugged enough to be him. From a few feet away, I heard, "What the hell are you doing?"

Jonah flashed a strong beam of light over me and Ray

Jenkins, who lay in a heap on the path next to me.

On my feet in an instant, I dusted my clothes and hands off, looked around, and then answered him.

"Where were you? I rushed over to meet you, and tripped over Ray instead. Is he dead, Jonah?"

"Let me have a look." He handed his flashlight to me, kneeled on one knee, and studied Ray.

I flashed light over the body and paused at the nasty gash on Ray's head. I shook when I saw the blood smeared on his face. Jonah stood up and made a call to the station requesting all and sundry to be dispatched to the scene. While I waited for him to finish speaking, it occurred to me that some of the people in Flora's journals were being disposed of one at a time. I shivered, shook my head at the seriousness of that thought, and gazed at the streets quickly filling up with emergency personnel.

I couldn't imagine who would commit such heinous crimes and in a town that prided itself on the image of friendliness and hospitality. I sighed and wondered if I'd made the right move coming to Schmitz Landing. My gaze fell on Jonah, and I knew I had.

He took my arm and drew me to the side of the path away from the gawkers, the rescuers, and his crime scene crew. The pressure of his grasp told me I was in for a tough night — I looked guilty, again.

"Go home, straight home. Don't talk to anyone. Do you understand me?" His words came out harsh and cold, chilling me to the bone. He gave me a light shove and turned to the rescue personnel who told us Ray wasn't dead, but badly injured.

I nodded and hightailed it away before Jonah changed his mind and arrested me on the spot for Ray's injuries. Even I could see that Ray hadn't fallen down and bumped his head, but instead, had been hit with a possible skull-crushing blow.

Unnerved and anxious, I ran up the studio stairs and locked myself inside. Jasmine and I watched the scene unfold across the green, not more than a hundred yards away.

I paced to release pent-up energy. The cat watched, her

steady gaze glued to me. I rubbed her head as I went back and forth past her. She made no sound, but waited with the patience only cats have. I envied her and wished for an abundant supply of the same.

Eventually I summoned the courage to leave my vantage point and headed into my living quarters. Flora's journal lay open on the chair where I'd left it. I picked it up, flipped to the page I'd been reading, and set about finishing it before I lost my nerve. Depressing as her words were, I hoped to find information leading to the one person who'd attacked two people, and killed Flora. Why I thought her words would reveal as much within these pages, I don't know, I just thought there might be a clue, if not an outright statement.

Maybe Flora didn't fear for her life. Maybe Janet didn't know what someone thought she knew. Why had Ray been smashed in the head? What was he aware of that would place him in jeopardy? He was a newspaper man with a far reach, one who knew how to acquire information — dirt really — on unsuspecting folks. Maybe I was reaching . . .

The last five pages of the journal explained a lot. Intent upon her revelations, I read the pages again and again, locking the information in the memory bank of my mind. I'd been mentioned several times from the middle of the book onward, but nothing pointed to me as a threat to Flora or anyone else. I was simply an itch that Flora couldn't scratch. She hadn't found out about me, and for that I was thankful.

The last five pages settled the matter of what she knew that would cause her undoing. She'd been stupid not to see where the information would lead her. I found it hard to believe what I read. Jonah needed to be apprised of what these pages contained.

Unable to fathom how the killer had managed to do what had been done to Flora, and possibly to Janet and Ray, I shook my head in disbelief. An accomplice was the only rational explanation, to my reasoning. Satisfied with the answer to the quandary, I flipped the last page and closed the book, smoothing the cover. I tucked it between the cushion and the side of the chair before walking to the studio to answer the door.

I stared at Jonah who stared back at me through the glass panes. Trepidation filled me as I opened the door to the lawman I'd fallen in love with. This could end badly for me, I just knew it. I wondered how I'd escape the wrath of the man whose temper sat so firmly on his face it made his scar intensely white. Now it stood out from where it creased the edge of his eye and brow. His face filled with questions, his eyes glistened like cold blue steel, and his body spoke of pent-up anger.

He strode in when I opened the door. His body tight, his voice cold, he shuttled me into the nearest chair and took the one opposite. This wasn't the box, but seemed an imitation of one, instead.

Jasmine meandered past us, took her place on a work table, and in one graceful move, settled next to my elbow.

Jonah glanced at Jasmine and then asked, "Where were you tonight after we parted?"

He was all business.

"I was here all evening until we were supposed to go to the park." As a crack attorney, Crystal had insisted I never elaborate, but keep my answers to a minimum. I'd listened and learned. Otherwise, I might have been imprisoned for crimes I'd never committed when Detective Brent had thrown a barrage of questions my way, time and time again.

Jonah made notes in his pocket notebook. "Did you see any movements on the green prior to leaving this house?"

I shook my head. "I was in the rear of the house all evening." I stroked Jasmine's silky coat and waited for his next question.

"Were you aware of anyone on the green tonight besides you and Ray Jenkins?" he asked in a softer tone. He measured me with his eyes, but his expression remained cool.

"No." I shrugged. "I didn't even see Ray until I tripped over him."

He jumped at my words. "So you knew it was Ray on the ground?"

My mistake. *Never relax and let your guard down.* Crystal's mantra echoed in my head.

"Not until I looked closer."

He gave a brief nod and scribbled notes again.

"When Ray was here earlier today, you had a confrontation, did you not?"

Oh crap. The tip of Jasmine's tail began to twitch.

"He made his intentions clear to me, and I asked that he not write an exposé on me. It wasn't a confrontation."

"You did tell me you lost your temper, though, didn't you?" His gaze never left my face. I struggled with the fact he'd use my own words against me.

I tried for a look of boredom. "That hardly means I killed him. Look elsewhere, Detective Kilbride." Jasmine's entire tail swished to and fro, the tip shaking a tad with each swish.

Unaware of Jasmine's angst, Jonah studied his notebook. When he'd finished, he looked at me and asked, "Did you assault Ray Jenkins, kill Flora Middly, and attack Janet Latchkey?"

Bracing myself, I answered, "No, I did not."

His manner relaxed, he said, "I found a few references to Ray and Janet in Flora's second journal. Did you know of Janet's connection to Flora?"

My mouth hung open, I gaped at him. "You're joking. They were connected? How?"

His lips compressed to a white line, then he snapped, "Do I look like I'm joking Katarina?"

"Not for a second. Do I?" I snapped back.

His lips twitched, but he held his peace and flipped a few pages further back in his notes. What the heck? Had he written a complete novel in there? I badly wanted to peruse his notes, but knew I'd never have the opportunity to do so.

Jasmine lifted a paw, set it back down, narrowed her eyes, and braced her body for attack. Placing my hand on her head, I held her neck and fingered the fur. She barely contained her need to protect me.

"Katarina, you look pretty guilty. You found Flora. Janet is taller than you and you have the strength to do her in. You and Ray had a disagreement, and when he was attacked not so very long ago, even though he insisted he slipped and fell, you also found him. A strap similar to the one found wrapped around Flora's and Janet's necks could have belonged to you. It looks bad for you," he warned with a hike of his brows and frost in his voice.

"Really? You really think I did the three of them?" I demanded with a snort. "No way, Detective Kilbride. Look somewhere else."

I'd wanted to offer up the last journal, but when it was time to come clean, and in light of Jonah's verbal attack on me, I refused to give him the book. Anger fought for an outlet as it raced through my veins. I wanted to reach over and slap him up the side of his head, to yell at him that I might know who'd done two of the deeds and possibly the third, but I figured he wouldn't listen.

Cops are like that. They get an idea in their heads and often won't let go of it. They rationalize why a person is guilty, how the crime came about, and like as not, you go straight to jail for something you had no hand in. In the meantime, a killer is on the loose, able to strike again at any moment, anywhere.

"Elsewhere?" His eyes narrowed to a slice of rich blue. "You keep repeating that. Do you want to share something that I need to know?"

His attitude had taken yet another turn. This time he sounded like the friendly Jonah I'd become used to, the one I looked forward to being with. 'Never be lulled into a sense of security where cops are concerned.' Crystal's words rang out loud and clear.

I offered an innocent question, "What do you think I would know, detective? I'm relatively new to Schmitz Landing."

He huffed and puffed like a dragon that'd lost his fire. It tickled my offbeat sense of humor to see him act out that scene in my head, but I kept the humor to myself.

He slapped the dog-eared booklet against the work table and focused on me with a hard-eyed stare. Jasmine stiffened, ready to pounce.

"If you're holding information that is imperative to this investigation, I'll toss your sweet ass in jail, Katarina. Make no mistake about it."

Before the cat could take revenge for his treatment of me, I uttered, "We're done. Leave, now."

"We're done when I say so, Ms. Granger."

His ominous tone set Jasmine off before I could stop her. She launched her attack, growling and making throat sounds that sent chills along my arms and up my spine. Before she could sink her claws into his face, Jonah raised his arm to fend her off.

I reached up, disengaged her from the sleeve of his jacket, and uttered cooing sounds in an effort to calm her.

Jonah slid off the stool, stuffed the notebook into his pocket, and uttered words to the effect that we weren't finished, and the next interview would likely be at the station.

"Bring it. I'll have my lawyer in tow, so don't think you can push me, Kilbride. Now, leave before I set the cat on you."

He stormed out. I quaked in my shoes at his threat until anger set in. I threw things, stamped my feet, cussed words my mother would never have thought I could possibly know, and then sat at the table and wept.

I don't cry easily. I'm a person whose chin juts out when the going gets bad. I'm persistent, and stubborn ... But enough already. I'd left Ohio to turn my life around, to start anew, in a place where nobody knew me or cared about my life back then. Now I'd become a suspect in not one, but three different situations. I sighed, flicked the flow of tears aside, and straightened the mess I'd made of the workspace.

There was only one thing left to do. Go to Gretchen's with the journal.

Chapter 19

I POUNDED ON Gretchen's door. She opened it a crack and mumbled something about it being midnight. I checked my wristwatch. It was way past that hour. I smiled and insisted she let me in.

Following her inside, I watched Gretchen stagger to the sofa, flop down, and lean her head on a pillow while dragging a bright-colored lap quilt over her body.

In a sleepy voice, she uttered, "This better be good. I have appointments back to back all day and I need sleep."

I produced the journal and watched her eyes pop open. She sat up so fast she almost threw herself to the floor as she reached for it.

"Flip to the last five pages," I recommended.

Paper fluttered as she furled the pages and asked, "Why?"

"Just do it."

"Okay."

I watched and waited while she read. When she'd finished the last line, the book slipped from her hands and she gawked at me in disbelief.

"Can't be," Gretchen uttered.

"Can, but not alone, I think."

"An accomplice? You think there's an accomplice?" She shook her head, her eyes filled with dismay.

"I do. It's the only way it all makes sense. Don't you agree?" I asked.

"*Criminy.* I wish I'd never read this. How do I get past these accusations pointed toward someone I've known for ages?"

"I feel the same way, but not knowing who the accomplice is makes me more uncomfortable." I sighed and then said, "Uh, by the way, Ray Jenkins was found bloody, but alive, by me, on the green tonight. I am suspect number one. Kilbride came by and drilled me for some time until I tossed him out. The cat attacked him, and now we're both in big trouble."

She brandished the journal she'd picked off the floor.

"Did you tell Jonah what you know about this?"

"Nope. He made me so angry that I refused to tell him what I'd learned. And ... before you insist I was wrong, I admit I should have given it to him."

Gretchen ruffled her heavy locks with her fingers and took a deep breath. "Then for cripes sake, get your butt over to his office and give it to him before something awful happens to you," she cried.

"I can't."

"Why not?" She tossed the offending reading material aside and spread her hands, palms up. "Why the heck not? Don't put your pride first. He'll be mad, but he'll get over it. Listen to me, will you? Things in this town are out of control. Somebody is bashing, choking, and killing people. I don't want you to be next."

Guilt riddled me, over holding out and the fact I'd now put Gretchen in danger. I mentally listed my options. I gave her a nod, tucked the journal inside my jacket, and muttered that I'd see her after work.

Gretchen walked me to the door and waited until I hit the entry level before she locked up. I heard the door close and the deadbolt click into place. I smiled. Knowing she was safe, I headed down the street at a trot.

Absent from class, Gretchen called between customers to ask if I'd taken her advice. When I didn't immediately answer, she gasped and ranted about how some people didn't know enough to smarten up, then abruptly disconnected the call. I guessed she was disgusted or angry with me. Either way, she'd have to get over it in her own time.

I had a mission, one that I'd set for myself on the way home from Gretchen's the night before. I spoke to the class when they first arrived, asking them to reserve their comments and thoughts on Ray Jenkins' hospitalization until we took our tea break.

Everyone agreed with a murmur or nod, and I started the class with a demonstration of an intricate tangle accompanied by an explanation of how to incorporate it into a larger illustration. Rapt attention and excitement cleared the gloom as everyone listened to my instructions and then began their version of the design.

Quietly, I walked the room to check on each rendering, and offered opinions when asked. I smiled, satisfied with the efforts of all, and left them to work out the remainder of their creations. About a half hour later, I put the kettle on to boil, set cups out along with the tea bag tin, a bowl of sugar, and the pitcher of milk.

It was time to begin my quest to establish how, why, and who had helped the criminal implicate me as the guilty party of three crimes. I wanted to know where the idea had originated and when they decided to implement their plan. Care was needed or I'd end up on a slab at the morgue. With caution, I chatted about finding Ray.

I let the class know that Kilbride had found me leaning over Ray, and that he'd questioned me mercilessly. I said I'd become his main suspect in all three deadly acts.

Her orange hair springing around her head, as though plagued by static electricity, Brenna Pestler slapped her pencil against the work table surface with a force I'd never witnessed before.

"I'll set him straight. Don't you worry, Katie," she blustered, her round face pinched with outrage. "How dare he think you could even harm a fly."

Bill chimed in, agreeing wholeheartedly with Brenna. Jill Crantz, whose thick hair braid dangled down the front right shoulder of her shirt, nodded and flung the heavy plait over her shoulder, whacking Francine Cross in the face with it.

Francine, hands already aflutter, swept invisible hair wisps off her face. "Katie, you don't mean Ray's attack, uh, you know, was like the others, do you?"

I nodded. "Similar. He was struck on the head. I don't think there was time enough to strangle him with a leather strap like Flora and Janet. This whole thing is so horrible."

Dramatically, I ran a hand across my forehead and sighed. I put on my best attempt at fear and said, "I think I might be arrested. Kilbride says it looks bad for me. I don't know what to do. I'm so worried. I've never had anything like this happen to me."

I watched the faces of all my students. Only Freda held my gaze. *She knew I lied.* How did she know? My pulse increased, my heart fluttered at the knowledge, and I turned my face away from the group.

In an instant, Freda reached across the table to assure me the culprit would be found, punished for the crimes, and that I shouldn't worry. Bill patted my shoulder. His large hand hit my scapula as though he petted a dog.

He commiserated with my plight. "Freda's right, not to worry. These matters have a way of working themselves out."

Simple words, but not always the case. I realized my mission would be more difficult than I'd anticipated. Had I really believed I would find the killer's accomplice just by putting out a few bread crumbs? Nah ... That would be too easy. I should have expected to work harder than this. Maybe I should have dropped entire loaves of bread instead of crumbs.

Who had the most to lose? What was the biggest and nastiest secret of all the ones Flora had ranted on and on about? I needed to know. I'd have to ask Jonah, which meant eating humble pie after the way I'd kicked him out the night before. Life can be miserable — and humble pie tasteless. *Blech!*

Our teacups empty, I waited for the students to return to drawing and then cleared the cups. I listened as soft words rounded the table while I washed the cups, watching from the corner of my eye, awaiting an odd expression on a face or a body language tell. I got nothing.

Disappointed, I began to discuss the upcoming town festival scheduled for the end of the month. I mentioned that the gallery show would be held at the same time and saw heads bob and smiles form on lips of all who'd participate.

"I plan to invite other people I've taught, to join us in displaying their work. We have a few weeks to get ready. If you're not working on projects at home, then you might want to start."

Questions flowed, answers were given, and our remaining time flew. The clock ticked twelve and the group broke for the day. As the last person exited, Gretchen scurried up the walk and burst into the classroom.

"I couldn't say much on the phone in front of my clients, but I wanted to let you know what I heard from my first customer this morning. She said Ray had been acquiring ads and told all his previous advertisers that he was writing an exposé on a famous person who lived here in town. Who do you think he meant?"

"I have a confession to make and may as well get it over with before you hear it from someone else," I mumbled as she tucked a strand of hair behind her ear.

Dumbfounded, Gretchen stared at me. "A confession?" she asked just above a whisper.

With only half her butt on a chair, Gretchen warned, "I don't like the sound of this. Go ahead."

I encapsulated my background, added the flight to New Hampshire as a new beginning and then told her Ray threatened to make my life's story front page news, adding at the end that Jeremy Bronson was supposedly at large. Her eyes grew wider and wider. I thought for a moment they would fall from their sockets.

Bounding from the chair, she yelled, "You've been holding

out all this time?"

I nodded and shrugged at once. "Sorry. I just wanted a fresh start without old baggage."

Her cheeks puffed outward as she blew a huge breath through puckered lips. I waited for Gretchen to process what I'd told her and cool down. I hoped that after her initial response she'd understand.

"I shouldn't have yelled. Sorry. I was surprised, is all. You went through a terrible ordeal. I can't blame you for wanting to run and hide. Geesh, Katie. Does Kilbride know?"

With a nod I explained how he found out. She grew pensive.

"He doesn't believe you killed Flora and jumped Janet or struck Ray, does he?"

"I'd have to say 'yes' at this time, but I'm on a mission to deliver the killer and their helper to him. I just need proof. I put out a few crumbs this morning and did an Oscar-winning performance to show how fearful I am of an imminent arrest. If it's thought that I'll be slapped behind bars, then a mistake might be made."

Gretchen checked the clock for time and started for the door. "I'll stop by after work. We'll talk then. I have to get back to the salon. See ya." I walked her to the gate, retrieved the mail from the post box, and watched Gretchen run the length of the street, meeting her client outside the salon. I waved when she glanced back. She lifted her chin in response and smiled as she herded the client through the door.

Wine sparkled in goblets. I passed one to Gretchen and sipped from the other. She'd arrived a bit after six, tossed her coat on a nearby chair and flopped onto the sofa, slipping her shoes off with a sigh of relief.

"Man, my dogs are tired. I've told Renee not to book me back to back, but she never listens. I feel so crushed for time when that happens." Gretchen chuckled as a wad of money fell from her pocket and plunked on the floor. "Good tips, though. When I gossip with the old biddies, they love it, and give me extra cash. I can hear their voices at the dinner table when they recount the happenings to their poor husbands." That said, she hiked her voice to a nasal pitch and imitated what she thought the women would sound like.

I laughed so hard I thought I'd bust a gut. She kept it up until I begged her to stop. Wiping the tears from my eyes, I took a huge swig of wine and nestled deep in the soft cushioned chair to chat.

"I've been thinking how to prove who our killer and helper are and that they did these crimes. It's driving me nuts. Gretchen, I can't come up with a scenario that won't put me, you, or anyone else in danger."

Gretchen gasped. "Don't include me in this. I'm scared enough just knowing about those stupid journals, without having everyone aware I might be privy to them. You can't think for a moment that I'd become your partner in crime ... again ... Do you?"

I stared at Gretchen. "I'm just saying that should we be in the same place at the same time, we would both be in danger if this person decides to take me on as the latest victim." I snorted. "I won't go down without a fight. You can bet the bank on that!"

"You said earlier that you'd offered crumbs to the students? What kind of crumbs?"

After a brief rundown, I said, "I can tell you this, Freda knew my history. When I said I'd never been a suspect before, she didn't utter a sound. The others were emphatic that I'd never hurt anyone, but not Freda. To cover her lack of emotion over my fears, she later assured me the culprit would be found. I'm not sure what to think where she's concerned."

Gretchen reached for the wine bottle, topped her glass, and slugged down a few mouthfuls of the sweet beverage. I guessed I'd scared the daylights out of her and she couldn't process all that I'd told her earlier in the day. Our minds can only hold so many revelations at once.

Tucking her folded legs beneath her, Gretchen lay back against the sofa. Deep in thought, she swirled the wine in her glass and stared at the liquid as it swished round and round. Snuggled against Gretchen's thigh, the tip of the cat's tail flicked ever so slightly.

A knock on the kitchen door sounded as Gretchen opened her mouth to speak. We stared at one another for a cool second or two before I jumped up to answer the summons. Jasmine's ears perked up, though she remained in place.

Exterior lights brightened the grounds. Jonah stood on the doorstep, waiting for me to let him in, which I did with serious reluctance and a heavy heart.

"Come in. Gretchen and I are having some of wine. Would you like a glass or is this official business?"

"No to both questions. I stopped in to make sure you're safe."

"Why wouldn't I be?" I glanced at Jonah. He looked at Gretchen and then at me again.

Hairs on the back of my neck stood to attention. Goose bumps riddled my skin and my heart raced like a Maserati at high speed.

Chapter 20

I ROUNDED ON Gretchen. *"You told him?"* I accused her. Jasmine stiffened, her ears flattened, her tail fluffed. She looked from me, to Jonah, and then settled her glare on Gretchen.

Wine spilled across her lap as Gretchen felt the prick of Jasmine's pointed claws. "Yow, cut that out." She pushed the cat aside, jumped from her seat, scooted out of reach, and rubbed her hand. "Get away from me you beasty girl."

I swept Jasmine up from the sofa, tucking her firmly under my arm, and murmured soft words to calm her. I figured she'd go into complete attack mode if I didn't get her under control.

"Wait right here, both of you," I commanded as I raced from the room to put Jasmine behind closed studio doors. Returning through the hallway, I heard her yowling complaint grow in intensity. She was as dangerous as any Rottweiler.

The thought brought a smile to my lips as I considered letting her loose on the two people awaiting me. Nah, not a smart idea, that.

Jonah and Gretchen sat side by side on the sofa in the cozy room. Soft firelight flickered as they whispered to one another. I had a clear view from where I stood in the shadowy corridor. When I reached the light, they stopped talking, and waited.

"When were you planning to tell me you ratted to Jonah?" I asked Gretchen.

"You've got it all wrong. I never said a word to him. Honest."

"Yeah, right. You wanted him to know from the beginning."

In relax mode, Jonah watched us, his eyes bright. He gently

brushed his scar. It was a sure sign he was thinking hard. But, thinking about what?

"Explain why you'd stop by to see if I was safe then?" I demanded of him.

"I'll ask the questions here," he answered. "You two have a secret, and you'll tell me what it is. Right now. Spill it, or you'll both end up at headquarters."

Threats, I loathe threats. Empty words, spoken to fill you with fear.

Fear. Another thing I detest. I'd have thought Jonah would realize by now that those two things failed to work on me.

I shot back, "Blah, blah, blah. Try again."

Jonah flew off the sofa. Stepping close, he towered over me and murmured softly, "Don't push me, Katarina. I will make good on that promise."

I inched close to him. I stared upward through the narrowed slits of my eyes. Burning anger roared through my body. "Don't push me either, Kilbride, or I'll make you sorry you ever met me. Remember this, I've taken on worse than you and survived. Don't make me repeat my actions."

Tight-lipped, he stepped back when Gretchen cleared her throat as a reminder of her presence. I relaxed a little and turned to Gretchen, whose face held a look of fascination. Her eyes bright, the beginning of a smile tickled the corners of her mouth.

"You two are volatile. Holy cow!" she breathed.

"Sorry for the outburst, Gretchen," Jonah said with a disarming half-smile. He tipped his head in my direction. "She can be pretty stubborn."

I bristled at the remark, but knew he was right. I refused to rebut the accusation and focused my attention on how he'd so adeptly trapped us in our own deceitful web.

Jonah once again planted himself on the sofa. He crossed his legs at his knees, smiled at each of us, and appeared to have regained composure. Only his eyes gave him away. His sharp, sparkling stare knifed through me before he turned the look to Gretchen.

"Let's try this again, but on friendlier terms, shall we?" he asked. "What are you holding back and why? I can help you, if you'll let me."

The silkiness of his voice reminded me of another detective, back in the day. He'd tried to cajole and charm me, then he'd threatened me, tried to trap me, turned my words around, and had used a whole bunch of other nasty ways — short of water boarding — to force me to confess to a crime I hadn't committed. I must admit though, Jonah was better at deception than Detective Brent had been. At least, he was more charming.

I threw my hands up in despair and plunked into my comfy chair. Gretchen rose and stood near the fireplace, rubbing her hands toward the flames as if she'd caught a chill. She looked worried.

"Tell him and get it over with," I said to Gretchen. "I'm tired of the whole affair, about what's happened, and what could." I yanked the journal from between the cushion and the chair arm where I'd stuffed it. I tossed it to Jonah and said, "Here, read this."

He caught it, looked at the journal, turned it over and exclaimed, "You held this back?"

"Not intentionally. I found it in the back of my closet. It must have slid between the shelf and the wall. When I took the others out to return them to their hiding place at Flora's, I thought I had them all. It wasn't until later I realized there was one missing."

His temper flared, his face turned hard, stone cold, and pure white. "That's no excuse," he roared. "It's been a while since you were at Flora's." Jonah stood, paced the room, slapping the leather journal against his leg as he moved. "Honest to God, you infuriate me. Do you know what a dangerous game you're playing?" he shouted.

I flung a hand outward, motioning to the seat he'd just vacated. "Oh, stop yelling and sit down or this conversation is over and you can figure things out by yourself."

From behind her hand, Gretchen gave a snort and sat cross-legged on the rag rug in front of the fireplace. She hid her smile from Jonah, but glanced at me, her eyes filled with laughter.

In a fraction of a second, Jonah had placed his hands on either side of the chair arms and bent so close to me his nose nearly touched mine. "I find no humor here and your attitude sucks. Smarten up, and grow the hell up, Katarina." He stepped back, resumed his seat, and glared at each of us in turn.

I drew a deep breath, slowly exhaled, and began to explain how we'd come to the conclusion that Flora had notes hidden in the house. I said we'd been surprised to find the journals and hadn't wanted to give them up once we'd taken them. By the time I finished describing what we'd done, how it had happened, and what I'd found out, Jonah was shaking his head in disbelief.

He'd managed to listen without interruption, but I knew he'd been hard pressed at times. That's what made him a good cop. He knew when to let his person of interest ramble on. That's how he proved them guilty.

So what if I'd admitted to breaking and entering, theft, breaking and entering a second time, and withholding information relevant to an ongoing investigation? Those were only misdemeanors, right? Since the theft was under fifteen hundred dollars, I'd likely get probation or maybe a year or two in the slammer, right? With a worthwhile, savvy attorney like Crystal, I'd walk. I knew it, as did Jonah, *if* he chose to pursue my indiscretions. Leery of the jail time aspect, I remained confident in Jonah's unwillingness to make an arrest.

He flipped through the pages and eventually asked, "Is there specific information in this journal I should look at rather than having to read all the filth written by a mentally disturbed woman?"

Gretchen told him to skip to the last five pages. He did so and scanned them quickly. At the last page, he glanced at us and then flipped back to the first of the five pages. He read slowly, taking in the implications, digesting them. Every now and then, he sighed, and shook his head. Finally, he looked at me and remarked, "This is rubbish."

Rising from the floor, Gretchen announced, "I'm making coffee. Anyone interested?" She threw me a roll of her eyes and headed toward the coffee pot.

I called out that I'd like some and that she should make enough for all of us. A mumbled reply I couldn't understand was all I got. With a shrug, my attention returned to Jonah.

"What else do you think besides 'its rubbish'?" I asked. "There's valid information in those pages. I'd say Flora was onto something big."

"What do you want me to say other than the fact that you've been foolish not to give this to me? How long have you known what these pages contained?"

"Not long. I read it a couple nights ago and then went to Gretchen's afterward. We talked it over." I shrugged. "She insisted I give you the book. You and I argued. I became angry and refused to take her advice until tonight. End of story."

"Listen to your friend in the future. It's plain that Flora thought she had a serious secret here and was about to blackmail someone or let the world know. Whether these accusations are true or not is another matter. I'll look into her allegations." He favored me with a hard look and said, "Until then, stay out of my investigation. Do you understand?"

Gretchen returned with a tray of filled-to-the-brim coffee cups and several pastries she'd found in my mother's antiquated glass pastry tray. We helped ourselves, ate and drank in silence, and started a new discussion on why Flora thought she could get away with tormenting so many citizens.

Gretchen blew a huge breath and said, "There's such an assortment of entries, I'm beginning to think Flora was seriously unhinged. They all can't be true, can they?"

I swallowed my last mouthful and said, "Some of them might have a smidgeon of truth, but others are surely from her imagination. She was paranoid. I knew that from dealing with her on a regular basis."

"When the other journals came to light, I dug through the

computer files at the station for complaints against Flora, or those filed by her." Jonah shook his head. "I was astonished at the number of reports that popped up. Her neighbors reported her harassment, and several local businesses did too. I couldn't believe how many people had reason to dislike her — or that she wasn't smart enough to fear for her life. She was pretty brutal when it came to annoying people."

I snorted. "I can attest to that. She came to the studio a couple times and made bold remarks, snide insinuations, and once even threatened me, but I sent her packing." I thought for a moment about her threat. At the time it hadn't meant much to me since I was so sure I'd covered my tracks.

I glanced up to find Gretchen and Jonah's eyes upon me. "What?" I asked.

Jonah smirked. "You have that *aha* look on your face. You know the one where, much to your surprise, the light goes on?"

Gretchen laughed and nodded. "You remembered something and know it's important, don't you?"

"Flora came here one day as class ended. The students were on their way out. She lingered, waiting until we were alone. I wasn't sure what she wanted, but I was wary. At first she made a few remarks to anger me, but I refused to go that route. When that didn't work, she said something to the effect that pasts catch up to us and how unsettling it can be. I thought she meant hers, not mine."

Jonah set his cup on the tray and asked, "Did she say anything else?"

The scene flickered through my mind. I shook my head. "She would have gone on, but someone entered the studio." The memory sharpened. I sucked in a breath. "It was Ray Jenkins. He stepped through the door, offered Flora a murderous glare, and gave her a wide birth. She did the same. I thought for a moment they were about to pummel one another. All of a sudden, Ray smiled at me, ignored Flora as though she wasn't there, and asked if I wanted to discuss an advertisement for the studio."

"How did Flora react?" Jonah wanted to know.

Gretchen leaned forward, waiting to hear more, her expression avid.

"She harrumphed, nearly snarled, and then stomped from the building. I could tell by Ray's attitude that he was pleased she had gone, though I didn't mention what had happened." I watched Jonah, wondering at his train of thought.

"So, there was definitely something wrong between those two. Did Ray ever talk about his encounters with Flora?"

With a shake of my head, I glanced at Gretchen. She made the same response.

"I don't ever remember Ray talking about his personal life, other than his news-reporting ambition." I gave Jonah a meaningful look, hoping he wouldn't mention the threat of exposure I'd received from Ray.

Jonah nodded. "I've asked around about Ray, but he kept to himself. The most everyone said about him concerned his work at the newspaper. It seemed he shared nothing of a personal nature."

Gretchen choked on her coffee and gasped for air. When she breathed normally, she glanced at Jonah and me and fiddled with her cup.

"Okay, spill it, I know you've got information," I demanded.

Her eyes pleaded that I not make her tell, but I ignored the plea. "Now, Gretch, give it up."

Reluctantly, she began. "Mary Smarten, the book store manager, came in once to have her hair colored. While she was there, Ray stopped by for the salon's ad placement. They looked at one another. He became nervous and hurried out of the shop as fast as he could. When he was out of sight, I mentioned how strange he'd acted. She smirked and said he was strange. She whispered to me that he was gay."

"Is that it?" Jonah asked.

"Well ... she said she'd seen him and his *friend* at the theater two towns over. She said they were more than hugging. I shrugged and said, 'To each his own.' That ended the conversation. She's never mentioned it again. I bet Flora knew. Small towns such as this often have specific views on morality, even though those same people have habits they themselves would like kept under wraps."

"If she knew, she never wrote it down," Jonah noted. "When was this, exactly?"

Gretchen tilted her head in thought. "It wasn't long before Flora's death. Sorry I didn't think of this earlier, but so much gossip is shared at the salon all the time — things like who is mad at whom, or who's been offended by another. I just didn't pay much attention to it."

Jonah gave her a nod. Sure, she'd be forgiven, but I'd be tortured for not remembering. Honestly, is there no happy medium here? I grimaced and rubbed my scalp with my fingertips, shook out my hair, and yawned.

The clock chimed the hour. Jonah's cell phone jingled and he answered it while he strode from the room. I looked to Gretchen as she yawned.

We were exhausted, both mentally and physically. I grinned, said we needed to resume our conversation in the morning, and handed her jacket to her.

With a promise to see me at class the next day, Gretchen readied to leave. Jonah offered her a ride after saying he had to return to the station. She agreed and they walked out together.

While retrieving a very put out Jasmine from the studio, I could see Jonah's car move away from the curb. Jasmine sniffed, turned her head away from me, and jumped to the floor from the top of the cash register. Her tail pointed straight up in the air, Jasmine marched past without a glance.

Jonah was right to be disgruntled. I had to admit that much. Was he correct in his assumption that Gretchen and I were in danger? What would happen next?

Flexing my shoulders to release the tension bunching my tendons and muscles, I meandered into the cozy room, flicking off lights as I went. Facing the fireplace, her back to me, Jasmine's cold-shoulder attitude was obvious.

Chapter 21

WARMTH FROM THE sun brightened my day as I shuffled the bed covers into place, picked my clothes off the floor, and watched Jasmine take in my actions from her spot at the end of the bed. I guessed all was forgiven when she hopped over to me and mewed loudly for attention. I stroked her silky smooth fur coat before I skipped downstairs with her in tow.

When our morning routine was done, I entered the studio, closed the hallway door and set to work. I had an hour or so before class commenced and figured it was about time I finished the drawing I'd kept covered from prying eyes. The work would have to go to the framer today in order for it to be ready for display during the next gallery show.

The drape slipped from the stand when I tugged the corner of it. I tossed the white cloth aside and stood back to view the rendering. All the design needed was additional shading. I smiled at the *oops* places I knew were unintended ink marks, satisfied no one else would know. That was one of the best things about tangling.

I chuckled and set about shading corners, lines, and crevices with graphite. Using the blending stump I smudged the graphite outward until it faded, making the important areas of the drawing pop forward.

I'd finished in time to re-cover the piece when I heard hoots of laughter from my students who ambled up the outside steps. I grinned and greeted them when they entered. It's funny how sunshine affects people. Sunny weather brings cheer, while rainy weather makes us feel dismal.

Freda was the last to climb the short flight of steps to reach the porch outside the studio. Holding the door, I waited for her to enter the room. Her hand gripped the silver lion's head atop her black cane. I'd never noticed this cane before and asked if it was new.

With a slight smile, Freda said, "No, it's been in the closet for a couple years now, and I thought I should use it. Like changing your shoes, you need to change canes."

The idea hadn't occurred to me, and I chuckled along with her. It was hard to believe she was one of Flora's blackmail victims as noted in the final pages of the last journal.

Pondering the thought, I closed the door, and lightly clapped my hands to gather attention. I requested they bring in their works for inclusion in the gallery show from home as soon as possible. Glee-filled faces and garbled responses met my request. With my hands in the air, I good naturedly pleaded, "Simmer down. One person at a time, please."

Brenna's round face was rosy and filled with unbridled excitement as she stepped forward. "I have six pieces stored at home. Can I bring them in tomorrow?"

"Sure. I'll put them in the gallery and we'll price them at that time," I told her.

Course hairs sprung loose from Brenna's hair clip, seeming electrified as her head bobbed up and down.

Bill sat with elbows propped on the work table in front of him and wondered aloud how many items each of them would able to display. Fearing he'd gone overboard with his own work, I asked how many he thought each student should bring in for sale.

He rubbed his clean-shaven jaw and said he figured wall hangings could be kept to ten or so pieces per person, but furniture and the like should be lower in number. He justified his answer with, "We'll need floor space for people to walk around and view the offerings."

I glanced at each student in turn, waiting for feedback.

Nods of agreement made the rounds. Relieved there wouldn't be a disagreement over who brought what, or that we'd have to have a conversation over the size and cost of the pieces, I approved the idea with a hearty grin.

Her hands quivering, Francine noted that when Brenna delivered hers, she'd also bring in the work she'd managed to finish at home. "You don't mind me coming in at the same time, do you, Katie? I wouldn't want to put you out."

Francine's nervousness was apparent in all she did. I would have been hard-pressed to say I minded, when in fact, I didn't mind at all.

"Don't worry about a thing, Francine. I'll be ready for you both. Just let me know what time you plan to arrive," I assured her.

Gretchen stated she'd only have the work she'd done in class to display, while Janet Latchkey said she and Bill would deliver theirs together over the weekend if they could. I gave a nod and smiled.

Janet, obviously sweet on Bill for years, hadn't made a move on him. After she'd ended up in the hospital, Bill began what I'd call an old-fashioned courtship of her. I smiled over their relationship, which until recently, had been virtually hidden from the rest of us.

I guessed Bill realized he'd nearly lost a good woman and regretted his earlier lack of attention where Janet was concerned. To say Janet had a soft spot in her heart for him was making light of her true feelings. Why he'd never noticed how much she cared for him was a mystery ... Or maybe he had known, and was afraid to act on his feelings.

Men can be idiots at the best of times. Take Jonah, for instance, he had no idea that I was head over heels in love with him. Then again, I figured I'd made my feelings abundantly clear earlier and he'd tried his best to ignore them.

Jill Crantz was the only student absent today. She'd left a message with Gretchen to the effect she had to work extra hours, and she would return to class as soon as she could get away. Jill had no completed work to enter in the gallery show, so I decided to enter my one and only illustration.

Lastly, Freda said she'd been hard at work on two larger pieces for the show. Her inventory of smaller items would fall into the ten or under category Bill had mentioned, and she'd deliver those after class one day that week.

I explained, despite their plans, the students could bring their work in anytime before three on any afternoon during the week. This meant I wouldn't have to hang around waiting, and I could enjoy some free time.

After the conversation dwindled, I watched tile designs take shape and develop depth. Each person had their own flare for tangling, every one different than the last. My heart swelled when I thought how far they'd come as a group, and as individual artists, while using the art form to handle their angst.

Class broke for the day. Sunshine streamed through the windowpanes and the open door as one by one the students departed. From the doorway, I watched Freda walk along the path toward the gate. When she reached the bench where Flora's body had been left for me to find, Freda stopped, studied the spot, and then glanced at me over her shoulder. The look in her eyes chilled me to my soul. With effort, I smiled and waved good-bye to her and turned away.

Francine hugged me as she stepped past. She wanted me to know that whatever gossip was going round about my finding Ray Jenkins in such bad shape in the park, the group knew I hadn't been the one to bash him in the head. She ended with, "He's in serious condition. Bleeding in his brain, I heard. He might not make it. The doctors have had him flown to a hospital in Boston."

Aghast at his condition — and the idea of gossip running rampant about how I may have done him in — I held my surprise in check and thanked Francine as she scurried out the door. I turned to find Gretchen flipping a pencil back and forth between her fingers.

"What?" I asked as I took in her solemn face.

"When will you face Freda down? I know it's on your mind. You're incredibly transparent, Katie."

In a snit, I answered, "I'm not transparent. I have no intentions where Freda is concerned. We don't know for certain if she's the guilty party or who her partners are or were. I've been wrongly accused of crimes, and I refuse to make accusations against someone, especially a frail woman like Freda. Just because Flora wrote that she'd tried to blackmail Freda by threatening to divulge her secret to all and everyone, doesn't mean it's true. Flora was a nutcase. You and I both know it!"

"Okay, okay. Don't get cranky." Gretchen waved her hands in the air. "I've got to go to work. I'll stop by later and we'll talk again. Don't be angry. I'm only concerned for you."

I fluffed fly-away wisps of hair off my face. Gretchen was a good friend, one that I'd never had before now.

I gave her a smile and said she should come by soon, so we could plan how to force Freda to tell us what Flora was using to blackmail Freda.

Gretchen chuckled in relief. "I'll see you later, then."

When the door closed, the cat howled her discontent at being locked away. I opened the hallway door to let her into the studio to keep me company.

Before lunch could be made and eaten, the room required straightening. In a matter of minutes, I'd organized books, tiles, notes, and had swept the floor. Jasmine watched from her perch on top of the cash register. Her whiskers twitched, the tip of her tail quivered as she gazed at me, but she never made a sound.

Just as I tucked the dustpan and brush neatly away in the small broom closet next to the restroom, the door chime sounded and the door opened.

Freda Grace stepped inside, one hand gripping the door handle, and the other tightly wrapped around the silver-handled cane. Her expression was serious and I waited with bated breath while she closed the door firmly behind her.

"H-have you brought your work for display?" I asked, glancing out the window to see if she'd left merchandise on the porch.

"No, Katie, I've come to set the record straight," Freda remarked dryly.

"W-what record? I d-don't know what you're talking about, Freda," I stammered.

Freda frowned. Her wired-rimmed glasses slipped down her nose. She peered at me over them. I'd watched her do that before, but had never been the recipient of the disdain that followed the action.

"It's clear to me that you're aware of Flora's blackmailing habit. Flora could have made her choices differently, but she chose poorly. Someone had to put a stop to her nonsense. I think you know who that person was, don't you, Katie? Or should I address you as Katarina. That's your true name, isn't it?"

I took a couple steps back to distance myself from her. Leery of her reasons for returning to the studio, I waited with a nod of acknowledgement to each of her questions.

A stranger to me, this new and scary Freda watched me, her eyes cool and calculating. Trapped and unable to escape her, I feared she'd do something foolish. What? I didn't know and couldn't begin to guess.

"How long have you known my name is Katarina?" I wanted to know if she'd heard gossip or if her knowledge came from elsewhere. Where that might be was a mystery to me.

"I heard it some time past, and then again when I was at the hairdresser's two weeks ago. I would never have made the connection until you began playacting here in the classroom about Detective Kilbride's intention to arrest you. Really, Katie, you should have known better than that."

I cleared my throat, and tried to smile. Would I be stupid to ask her questions? I had nothing to lose and hoped Jonah might make an impromptu visit.

"What exactly do you think I know, Freda?"

She smirked. "You have no idea who I am, do you, my dear?"

"Uh, no, other than you're an upstanding citizen in this town and highly thought of by those who know you. Who should I think you are?" I asked.

"We'll get to that later. Right now, I want you to understand what happened to Flora — and why."

"If you want to share, by all means, go ahead." I motioned with my hand for her to sit across from me.

Freda shook her head, stayed put, and started her story.

"Flora Middly was the unkindest person I ever met. She would turn on a person in a second, even those you'd think she held dear. Francine is her daughter, you know. Flora became pregnant by the original owner of your house. He tricked Flora into thinking they would wed. Being young and naïve, Flora fell hard for him. After he'd bedded her, he walked away as though she didn't exist.

"Pregnant and scared, she went to a home for wayward girls, had Francine there, and later passed her off as the niece of a relative who'd died on the operating table. Francine never knew about her parentage until she was fifteen years old. She found out by mistake — the revelation leaving her the nervous wreck she is today. Flora was mean to her. Flora was bitter and wretched over the way she'd been treated by her own family, and she treated Francine the same way." Freda stepped closer to me, leaned on her cane, and eyed me with a cold glare.

"Too bad, Katie, that you couldn't stay out of Flora's affairs." Freda sniggered. "I realized you were aware of my involvement in Flora's death when you performed your act in class. You had everyone fooled, but me, of course." This new and terrifying version of Freda glanced around and continued.

"But, I digress. Francine's personal affairs aren't why I'm here, though I thought you should know who she really is. We all have things we'd rather others didn't know about us. Surely you're aware of that, more than most. Am I right?"

I nodded and said nothing. I wouldn't still her ramblings for anything in the world. I glanced away from her for a second and noticed Jasmine was stiff, unmoving, like a stuffed animal.

Once again, I turned my attention to Freda Grace — a mere slip of a woman whose frail appearance could fool even the shrewdest person I knew. It was difficult to envision her strangling Flora or Janet.

"Why did you really settle here?" Freda asked.

I thought back to my earliest recollection of the town and said, "Honestly, I found the area delightful, the townsfolk friendly, and I needed to make a change."

"You came here purely by accident, then?"

"I did," I answered. "I stumbled on a magazine ad when I toured this state. The realtor showed this house to me and it was love at first sight. I have no idea what you're getting at Freda. Do you think I had an ulterior motive for moving to Schmitz Landing?"

Slowly, she shook her head. Whether it was at my stupidity, naiveté, or if she was rethinking her situation, Freda came to a decision.

"You're a lovely girl, Katie. However, I can't take the chance that you won't turn me over to the police."

"Why would I do that, Freda? I have no idea what you're going on about." Aware the ploy probably wouldn't work, I gave it a try anyway.

Freda brushed my words away with a flick of her hand. "Please don't play dumb. It doesn't become a bright, talented, and shrewd girl such as you. I faced Flora with courage when she tried to blackmail me. She didn't have the whole truth, but she was close enough that I feared she'd find out all of it. She wanted me to pay her an unseemly sum of money on a regular basis in order to still that rotten wagging tongue of hers."

"What do you think she knew that was such a threat to you, Freda?" I asked in a soft voice.

"Initially, Flora made snide remarks, hinting at your connection to my family. How she'd put it together amazed me, but I put off paying her. Affronted because I wasn't afraid of her, she became angry, and wanted to hurt me. Little did she know, she couldn't hurt me more than my own family had managed to. I wouldn't stand for her miserable attempt to extort my meager savings from me."

"What connection do I have to your family?" My parents

had never mentioned relatives living here in New England.

"My nephew was your boyfriend for a time. He told me of your artistic talent, the way you enjoyed life, and how great a person you were. He was right, too. Unfortunately, he wasn't the best apple in the barrel. He had a bad streak in him, just like his father did. Jealous of what others had and he didn't, Jeremy would steal from them when they least expected it. He had charm, but underneath, he was rotten to the core."

Astounded by her disclosure, I choked at her words. It couldn't be true, it couldn't. I'd have known about his family, wouldn't I? Except, he hadn't really spoken of them much. He'd mentioned living in Jersey, as in New Jersey, not New Hampshire.

I whispered, "Jeremy Bronson is your nephew?"

Freda nodded. Her eyes held a glint of satisfaction over my reaction. I was dumbfounded and shocked by her admission.

Her fingers worked the silver head of the cane as she rubbed them over the slick surface of it. Freda declared Jeremy had come to her home after he'd broken off our relationship. He'd had small works of art tied to his motorcycle and had said he had more in a storage unit in Jersey. When Freda demanded to know where he'd gotten them, Jeremy had lied and said he'd won some pieces in a poker game, and the rest he'd bought.

Freda shook her head in disgust, and added, "That's when I figured out he'd been up to no good. I went to see my cohort, Ray Jenkins. I asked him to dig up what he could on crimes in Columbus, Ohio during the time my nephew was there. You and your family topped the list of violent crimes. I'm sorry for what you went through back then, but I can't take a chance on you now."

Stunned, I asked, "You and Ray are buddies?" Freda's confession was becoming weirder by the moment.

She offered me a kind smile. "Of course he is, dear." She pointed to her own small frame. "How could I have managed to murder fat Flora and attempt to take the life of a woman as tall as Janet?" Freda made a sound with her tongue against her gums and teeth.

She admonished me, "You need to keep up, dear. Ray had his own issues with Flora. When I spoke with him about Jeremy's possible crimes, we devised a way to get rid of Jeremy. Then we worked out a way to dispense with Flora. That took longer than I expected, but she got what was coming to her in the end. I do apologize for implicating you, but I had to lay the blame on someone." Freda shrugged and fell silent.

Angry, I glared at Freda. "Let me get this straight, you had Ray strangle Flora and leave her on my bench so I'd be suspected of murder?" My voice had begun to rise. I noticed Jasmine's tail twitch slightly. The rest of her body was rigid and her eyes never left me for a second.

Freda inched closer. "Dear, don't be upset. It's bad for you. But then, you of all people know anxiety is unhealthy for you. Am I right?"

The woman had lost her cookies, marbles, senses, and everything else I could think of. She was deranged, a veritable psychotic woman. I also realized I was in serious danger. I felt it all the way to the marrow of my bones.

I nodded, and prompted her to tell me more. "Why was Janet next on your list?"

"I was worried Janet had heard me talking to Ray one day when we were in the park. She used to get a morning coffee, cross the green, and then come to class. I wasn't aware she was behind us until she greeted Ray and me. One must be aware, and beware, you know. It doesn't bode well to become sloppy. I persuaded Ray of his need to take care of her.

"He didn't want to at first, but I can be very convincing when I need to be." Satisfied that she'd been smart in having Ray attempt to kill Janet, she leaned heavily on her cane, a smug look on her face.

When she opened her mouth to speak, my phone rang. I'd left it on the table instead of in the charger and held up a finger for Freda to wait. I jumped forward to take the call. Surprised at my nerve, Freda moved a bit closer. I stepped away as I spoke into the receiver and Freda backed off. Sure she was only dealing with half her wits, I figured I had nothing to lose by answering the call.

"H-hello?" I murmured, pressing the phone tight against my ear. I wasn't about to let Freda know who was on the other end of the call.

"Hey Katie, Jonah here. I'll be stopping by in a while to see you. I have news of Ray's condition. Before I forget to tell you, remember that sweet smell of Janet's attacker that had me stumped? It seems Ray has diabetes, and when his blood sugar isn't under control, he emits that odor. I was quite surprised when I found out. Anyway, how about some dinner at the café later?"

Another piece of the puzzle fell into place. I said, "I see, well, I have a guest right now, but you can deliver on Friday."

"Friday? It's Monday," Jonah answered and then he became silent. He murmured softly into the phone, "Are you all right?"

"Listen, I have to get back to my company. Remember, you can deliver that merchandise on Friday." I emphasized the first half of the word Friday in hope Jonah would take the hint that I meant Freda. It sounded silly, even to me, but I was fast on the path to desperate.

Her cane scraped the hardwood flooring as I abruptly disconnected the call. The hard soles of Freda's shoes clapped against the wood when she stepped closer to me. I turned as she raised the cane high above her, and swung it at my head.

What followed is still unclear. Everything happened at the speed of light, or so it seemed. I batted at the metal handle of Freda's cane, causing it to strike my collarbone. I heard a crack, but I was in motion and didn't heed the sound, or the pain.

Jasmine chose the same moment to launch an attack on Freda. Her claws exposed, a loud growl emitted from her throat as Jasmine sank her pointy hooks into the flesh on Freda's neck and face.

I stumbled against the table, shoving it aside as I fell, and tumbled into the storage cabinet, thumping my head against the corner of it. Woozy, I heard Jasmine snarl and Freda scream at the same time.

Freda, agonized with pain, thrashed in an effort to fling the cat away from her. Jasmine's triumphant attack continued until I crawled toward the two females writhing on the floor.

Freda's arms flailed and blood spattered as she beat the cat off her. Jasmine had etched deep claw marks into Freda's face. Freda was a bloody mess by the time I wrenched the cat off the old woman.

Blood smeared Freda's usually impeccable coiffure, it soaked into the collar of her blouse and jacket, and splattered on the floor. Her whimpers left me rattled, but I was unwilling to approach the crazed woman. Instead, I cringed against the cabinet, clutching the feral feline tightly against my body.

I sidled to where I knew she couldn't reach me and insisted, "Where is Jeremy, Freda? What happened to him?" I know, it was cold of me to be so cruel to Freda, but the threat of Jeremy was all I could think of at the moment.

She turned her bloody face toward me and mumbled, "He's in the basement." Her eyes closed, and she passed out. I watched her chest rise and fall, nervous that she'd die of a heart attack before Jonah arrived. And I had no doubts he would arrive any second.

Sirens blared louder as they drew near. I rested against the cabinet with Jasmine in my arms. Her heart beat fast and hard against my body. I soothed the cat that'd fought off my attacker like nobody else ever could.

Chapter 22

MY FRONT DOOR swung open with enough force that it slammed against the wall with a loud bang, rattling the glass windowpanes. When I clutched Jasmine closer, pain shot across my collarbone, up my neck, and into my face.

Jonah rushed inside, followed by Gretchen. At the scene in front of them, both my rescuers stopped short. Jonah looked at Freda and then at me.

"Is she dead?" he asked.

"No, just out cold. Jasmine came to my defense when Freda tried to club me to death after I got off the phone with you. She confessed to the murder of Flora, the attempted murder of Janet Latchkey, and I'm certain she clubbed Ray, too." Ravaged by a new onslaught of pain, I glanced at the disarray of the once neat studio.

I asked with a whine in my voice, "Can somebody help me off the floor? I think Freda cracked my collarbone."

Jonah took my right arm while Gretchen hauled me up by the belt loop on my slacks. Jonah ordered a rescue be dispatched to my address and within a matter of minutes, emergency personnel filled the room.

I observed their treatment of Freda and listened to the offer of a lift to the hospital for an x-ray to my neck and shoulder. About to refuse — since I wouldn't ride with the same woman who'd just tried to kill me — Jonah interrupted and stated he'd see me to the hospital by way of his cruiser.

The rescue team left with Freda strapped to a stretcher. I

set Jasmine on the floor. She scooted into our living quarters. I smiled at the ferocious feline, but leaned against the counter as dizziness descended.

Jonah barked an order for Gretchen to get me some whiskey as I slid back to the floor, landing on my butt. Still conscious, it was plain I'd become the victim of an adrenaline rush. Once my adrenalin ran its course, all energy was sapped from my body.

I quickly slugged down the harsh liquor, coughing as it burned its way into my stomach. I felt the flames of it lick at my insides, and knew I'd feel better in a moment or two.

Jonah pulled my shirt aside to see if bone protruded through the skin. When his eyes widened, I knew he'd seen the scars Jeremy's attack had left on me. I turned my face away and said to Gretchen, "Why were you on Jonah's heels?"

She laughed. "I heard the siren, saw him flash past the salon, and just knew you were in trouble. I left my client with a perm in her hair and ran as fast as I could to get here." Gretchen glanced at her watch. "Gotta go or the woman won't have any hair left. Will you be all right? I can call and have my boss finish up for me, if you need me to stay."

Grateful for her offer, I told her to return to work and let Jonah take care of me. She grinned, agreed, and left.

"Tell me what happened?" Jonah demanded in a light tone as he hauled me off the floor once more.

We slowly walked into the living area. I explained what had transpired and how shocked I was to hear Freda was Jeremy's aunt. I ended with her confession that Jeremy was in her cellar.

I looked at him and asked, "Why would he be there?"

His grimace was enough for me to figure out that Jeremy wasn't living in the cellar — rather he was probably buried there. Shock set in at the idea and I flopped, weak-kneed, into the nearest chair. Pain shot through my system, and I told Jonah I would need to go to the emergency room.

My injury was mild in comparison to what Jasmine had inflicted on Freda.

The drive in the cruiser didn't take long and Jonah kept

looking at me sideways as he drove. He called ahead and let them know we were on the way and even put the light and siren on as we drove.

Jonah left me in the care of the emergency room staff while he went in search of Freda, who was apparently being treated for multiple lacerations. He smiled at me as he left the curtained enclosure where I lay on a gurney, and said, "I'll be back shortly. Stay put."

An hour later, I'd been patched up by an intern who told me 'I'd be right as rain in no time.' I waited for Jonah to return. The time dragged until I wondered if the good detective had left the hospital without me. I caught the attention of a nearby nurse, and asked if she'd check to see if Jonah was in with Freda Grace. The nurse assured me she'd do so and would return shortly.

Moments later, Jonah strode into the waiting room where I'd settled to wait. He took the chair next to mine, and asked if the doctor released me from care. When I nodded, he said he'd take me home.

On the ride home, Jonah said he'd gotten a statement of sorts from Freda. The woman had become incoherent, rambling on about the horrific crimes she and Ray has conspired to commit. Freda had been the thinker and Ray had been the doer. I shivered at the news.

Once in the driveway, Jonah insisted he'd come in for a bit and he stayed until I fell asleep. I was medicated for pain and soon fell into a deep sleep.

I awoke to Gretchen's snoring. No romance in that.

She lay sprawled on the sofa, an afghan draped across her chest, and Jasmine cuddled in the crook of her legs. I was curled into my comfy chair in the cozy living room, across from Gretchen. When I shifted my weight I swiftly regretted it. I felt like I'd either been hit by a train, or apparently I wasn't 'right as rain' quite yet.

I listened to the kitchen door open and close. Jonah strolled in holding a bag. He said fresh donuts were the doctor's orders, and I should consider the personal delivery a plus. I chuckled, waited for the coffee to perk, and then indulged in the sweetest tasting donuts I'd had in ages.

Jonah took a chair and faced me. He studied his fingernails, rubbed his scar, gawked at the furnishings in the room, and nearly drove me mad with his silence.

Finally he leaned forward and said, "We found Jeremy's body. I had to wait for a search warrant before we could search Freda's house and break up the concrete floor. Ray and Freda were very busy people."

Jonah sipped the coffee and continued. "Ray must have had one hell of a workout breaking the concrete flooring, burying Jeremy, and then pouring wet concrete over the body. If anyone had accused Freda, I would never have believed it, but obviously Flora knew Freda had a secret and wouldn't let her off the hook. That's why Freda and Ray killed Flora. She knew too much — but not quite enough."

With a nod, I filled him in with what I knew about the attack on Janet and why it had taken place. "When I had asked Janet to act out the attack with me, she was unwilling to relive the event. I know Janet never heard what they were discussing in the park or she'd have said. Freda refused to take any chances, insisting she couldn't be careless."

We talked the whole mystery out until we were satisfied we knew all that had taken place. Jonah mentioned Ray was still in a Boston hospital and would be transferred to a nursing facility. He hadn't yet regained consciousness, and the likelihood was he probably wouldn't, so he could escape trial for his part in the crimes committed.

Freda faced jail time, even at her age, for her part in things.

Jonah's blue-eyed stare traveled my face and moved over my body. "You'll never have to worry about any of them again. Not Jeremy, or Freda. Should Ray come back to life, he'll face worse charges than Freda, and you won't have to worry about him either." He leaned forward, kissed my forehead, and moved his lips to my mouth.

A loud *'ahem'* broke the spell and I smiled at the disgruntled look on Jonah's face.

Gretchen snickered and said, "I'm here in the room, in case anyone's interested."

Jonah smirked at me and remarked over his shoulder, "Don't you have to go to work?"

Her sudden flight from the sofa delighted both Jonah and me. We laughed as she raced around the house grabbing her belongings, and then ran out the door saying she was late for work.

I tried to rise from the chair. Jonah pressed me back into the soft cushions.

"There's no class for you today. I put a sign on the front door saying the studio was closed for a few days. I didn't think you'd mind," he said with a wide grin.

"You're right," I said. "I need time to figure things out. I'm not sure what to do, or where to take my life from here."

His eyes cool as he regarded me, Jonah sat back. "Are you considering leaving Schmitz Landing?" he asked.

I tried to shrug, but the effort was too painful. "I'm not sure what I'm going to do. My emotions are jumbled at the moment. I just need some time to sort them out."

His eyebrow hiked and an unreadable expression covered his face as he rose. Jonah cleared his throat and said, "I see. Well then ..." His voice trailed off as he strode to the door. He wished me a good day, and asked that I stay in touch. Then he was gone.

Chapter 23

LEAVES SPROUTED, FLOWERS bloomed, and life was nearly perfect for Jasmine and me at Tangled Wings Studio. I realized I finally had closure regarding the deaths of my parents and my own attack. Though the incidents had brought back painful memories, I'd never have to worry about Jeremy Bronson's whereabouts again. Crystal and I had spoken on the phone. She'd been relieved to hear that, as a threat, Jeremy was no longer an issue.

My students had feared I'd close the studio and leave town, but I was embedded in the community now, and I wanted to remain here. I assured them I was here to stay. The only person I hadn't assured was Jonah.

Unsure of the reason I hadn't called and asked him to come by, I needed to finish what I'd started where he was concerned. I wanted him in my life. There was no doubt in my mind about that. But I was unclear whether Jonah wanted to have a relationship with me.

Business had doubled, students flocked to fill classes, and my regulars arrived daily, excited to learn new tangling techniques.

A couple of college graduates had taken over reporting news in the *Schmitz Daily* rag. Ray Jenkins had survived and awakened from his head trauma, but wasn't ever going to be well enough to even dress himself, let alone live a normal life. His brain injury had been extensive, the doctors said.

With the sun on my back, I sat in the backyard on the bench by the river. A soothing breeze ruffled my hair and tickled my sense of smell with the sweet scent from pine trees that straggled the river's edge. The fresh woodsy smell left me feeling better than I'd felt in a very long time.

Relief from my past, lies confessed to, and a general sense of well-being possessed me. Only one thing remained unresolved. Telling Jonah of my feelings for him.

Jonah had been absent from my life since the day I'd commented on my need for time for decision-making concerning my future. I wondered whether he was giving me the time I'd said I needed, or if he'd decided to walk away from me. Either way, I hadn't stayed in touch with him as he'd asked. Maybe that's why he hadn't stopped by or called. I feared I was destined to live alone with my ferocious feline.

During a classroom exercise, I'd heard a couple of the students discussing the court case involving Freda and Ray. It seemed Jonah was up to his ears in evidence. A picture of him buried up to his ears in paperwork brought a smile to my lips as I knew that, like most cops, Jonah detested the reports that were such a standard part of police work.

An eagle soared, plunged toward the river, and swept a fish from beneath the surface. A tall shadow cast itself across me. Startled, I turned. Jonah stood near. His gaze took in the river, the eagle, and then landed on me.

"I knocked at the door. When you didn't answer I took a chance that you might be here by the river," he said in a thoughtful voice. "We need to talk, Katie."

"I was just thinking of you," I admitted. "We do need to talk." I'd risen from the bench and joined him. Together we walked toward the house where Jasmine waited for us. She sat in the kitchen window, staring as we ambled across the yard. My heartbeat quickened and my nerves sang. Good or bad, this was my one chance to tell Jonah what he meant to me.

Inside, Jasmine rubbed her head against Jonah's outstretched palm before she scooted off to the sun-filled studio. I closed the door behind her. Jonah and I stood a few feet apart in the kitchen. A heady breeze flowed through the open windows and fluttered the curtains.

Neither of us uttered a word for a few moments, and then we both tried to speak at once. Jonah's sudden laughter filled my heart with joy. I had to have this man in my life full-time. Nothing less would suffice.

His eyes sparkled with humor as he said, "You first, go ahead."

"I need you in my life. Not as a friend, but as more than that. I ca ..."

My words were blocked as his mouth came down on mine. He held me close, so close I thought our skin had melded into one body. He kissed me, long, deep, and hard. I'd never felt so alive in my life. I couldn't get enough of him.

My hands fumbled with his shirt buttons, working their way to his jeans. He pulled back, peered into my eyes with his passion-filled blue eyes and murmured, "Are you sure?"

"Damned straight, I am. Never more sure than now." With that, I slipped my clothes off and we made love on the kitchen table. From there, we moved to the sofa, the rug in front of the fireplace, and up to the bedroom.

Sated, I lay in a jumble of pillows and turned to catch him staring at my body. My scars fascinated him, just as his lonely scar had always fascinated me. Slowly, he traced each scar with the tip of his index finger — his touch as light as butterfly wings against my skin.

"You are lovely," he whispered.

"Why didn't we do this before? I've wanted you for so long," I breathed against his lips.

"The job," Jonah muttered. "It kept me away from you when all I could think of was you, touching you, making love to you, having you all to myself. You'll never know how hard those times were for me, to walk away when you invited me with your eyes and lips, to take you for myself."

I traced the muscles on his chest with the tips of my fingers. "Then tell me exactly why you didn't. I can't accept it was just your job that stood in your way."

"Remember when we had an argument about why you left

Columbus and why I left New York?" he asked.

I nodded.

"I'd gotten personally involved with a confidential informant who was killed in the crossfire when we took down the crime ring she had tipped us to. It was never clear who accidently shot her since the bullet went through her body and was never found. Whether it was me or the other detective working the case, we'll never know."

Jonah sighed. "Anyway, I left the department shortly after the incident. I couldn't deal with New York City crime any longer and wanted a quieter lifestyle. I'd found the ad for this job with the Schmitz Landing department and decided to give it a try."

"Were things working well for you here?" I murmured against his chest.

I felt his laughter before I heard it.

"Yes, until you moved to town. I'd heard about you, seen you from a distance, and at the various functions held by the community. I'd promised myself to never become involved, romantically or otherwise, with anyone, ever again. Then you found Flora, and I found you irresistible." He brushed a lock of hair from my face and said, "I never did ask you, but when you and Gretchen read the last few pages of the journal, who did you think Flora was intent on ruining?" He stroked my arm where it lay across him. His touch thrilled me, awakening the desire I'd felt only moments ago.

"I wasn't exactly sure who it was, Flora's writings were an bit vague. I just knew if I put out enough bate in my class, I'd get a response. I figured one of the students might know something. I won't be doing that ever again, I promise. During class, I said that I thought you planned to arrest me. The only person slow to react to the news, was Freda. I knew then that she was guilty, but I couldn't prove it. Gretchen wanted me to goad her in a confession, but I refused." I peered into his face and chuckled. "Since I'm so irresistible, I take it that you'll not be walking away from me, then?"

"Absolutely not! I'm here to stay," he answered in between the kisses he laid against my skin.

I smiled, wrapped my leg across his and let him have his way with me.

The End

Printed in the USA
CPSIA information can be obtained
at www.ICGtesting.com
LVHW050718120823
755033LV00034B/300